KU-656-061

Neil Gaiman has spent his adult life making things up and writing them down. He lives more in America than he does anywhere else. He has written books and films and children's books and television. He has a blog over at www.neilgaiman.com. He's won more than his fair share of literary awards, was voted twenty-first equal on a recent poll of Great British Authors, and has no idea where he put his keys.

Neil Gaiman
STARDUST

**headline
review**

First published in Great Britain in hardback 1999
by HEADLINE PUBLISHING GROUP

First published in Great Britain in paperback in 2007
by HEADLINE REVIEW
An imprint of HEADLINE PUBLISHING GROUP

This edition published in 2007
by HEADLINE REVIEW

1

ISBN 978 0 7553 3755 2 (A format)
ISBN 978 0 7553 3751 4 (B format)

Typeset in ZapfEllipt by Avon DataSet Ltd,
Bidford on Avon, Warwickshire

Printed and bound in Great Britain by
Mackays of Chatham plc, Chatham, Kent

Headline's policy is to use papers that are natural, renewable and
recyclable products and made from wood grown in sustainable
forests. The logging and manufacturing processes are expected to
conform to the environmental regulations of the country of origin.

HEADLINE PUBLISHING GROUP
An Hachette Livre UK Company
338 Euston Road
London NW1 3BH

www.reviewbooks.co.uk
www.hodderheadline.com

For Gene and Rosemary Wolfe

Song

Go, and catch a falling star,
  Get with child a mandrake root,
Tell me, where all past years are,
  Or who cleft the Devil's foot,
Teach me to hear mermaids singing,
  Or to keep off envy's stinging,
      And find
      What wind
Serves to advance an honest mind.

If thou be'est born to strange sights,
  Things invisible to see,
Ride ten thousand days and nights,
  Till age snow white hairs on thee,
Thou, when thou return'st, wilt tell me
All strange wonders that befell thee,
      And swear
      Nowhere
Lives a woman true, and fair.

If thou find'st one, let me know,
  Such a pilgrimage were sweet,
Yet do not, I would not go,
  Thou at next door we might meet,
Thou she were true when you met her,
And last, till you write your letter,
      Yet she
      Will be
False, ere I come, to two, or three.

         — John Donne, 1572–1631

Chapter One

In Which We Learn of the Village of Wall, and of the Curious Thing That Occurs There Every Nine Years

There was once a young man who wished to gain his Heart's Desire.

And while that is, as beginnings go, not entirely novel (for every tale about every young man there ever was or will be could start in a similar manner) there was much about this young man and what happened to him that was unusual, although even he never knew the whole of it.

The tale started, as many tales have started, in Wall.

The town of Wall stands today as it has stood for six hundred years, on a high jut of granite amidst a small forest woodland. The houses of Wall are square and old, built of grey stone, with dark slate roofs and high chimneys; taking advantage of every inch of space on the rock, the houses lean into each other, are built one upon the next, with here and there a bush or tree growing out of the side of a building.

There is one road from Wall, a winding track rising sharply up from the forest, where it is lined with rocks and small stones. Followed far enough south, out of the forest, the track becomes a real road, paved with asphalt; followed further the road gets larger, is packed at all hours with cars and lorries rushing from city to city. Eventually the road takes you to London, but London is a whole night's drive from Wall.

The inhabitants of Wall are a taciturn breed, falling into two distinct types: the native Wall-folk, as grey and tall and stocky as the granite outcrop their town was built upon; and the others, who have made Wall their home over the years, and their descendants.

Below Wall on the west is the forest; to the south is a treacherously placid lake served by the streams that drop from the hills behind Wall to the north. There are fields upon the hills, on which sheep graze. To the east is more woodland.

Immediately to the east of Wall is a high grey rock wall, from which the town takes its name. This wall is old, built of rough, square lumps of hewn granite, and it comes from the woods and goes back to the woods once more.

There is only one break in the wall; an opening about six feet in width, a little to the north of the village.

Through the gap in the wall can be seen a large green meadow; beyond the meadow, a stream; and beyond the stream there are trees. From time to time shapes and figures can be seen, amongst the trees, in the distance. Huge shapes and odd shapes and small, glimmering things which flash and glitter and are gone. Although it is perfectly good meadowland, none of the villagers has ever grazed animals on the meadow on the other side of the wall. Nor have they used it for growing crops.

Instead, for hundreds, perhaps for thousands of years, they have posted guards on each side of the opening on the wall, and done their best to put it out of their minds.

Even today, two townsmen stand on either side of the opening, night and day, taking eight-hour shifts. They carry hefty wooden cudgels. They flank the opening on the town side.

Their main function is to prevent the town's children from going through the opening, into the meadow and beyond. Occasionally they are called upon to discourage a solitary rambler, or one of the few visitors to the town, from going through the gateway.

The children they discourage simply with displays of the cudgel. Where ramblers and visitors are concerned, they are more inventive, only using physical force as a last resort if tales of new-planted grass, or a dangerous bull on the loose, are not sufficient.

Very rarely someone comes to Wall knowing what they are looking for, and these people they will sometimes allow through. There is a look in the eyes, and once seen it cannot be mistaken.

There have been no cases of smuggling across the wall in all the Twentieth Century, that the townsfolk know of, and they pride themselves on this.

The guard is relaxed once every nine years, on May Day, when a fair comes to the meadow.

***

The events that follow transpired many years ago. Queen Victoria was on the throne of England, but she was not yet the black-clad widow of Windsor: she had apples in her cheeks and the spring in her step, and Lord Melbourne often had cause to upbraid, gently, the young queen for her flightiness. She was, as yet, unmarried, although she was very much in love.

Mr Charles Dickens was serializing his novel *Oliver Twist*; Mr Draper had just taken the first photograph of the moon, freezing her pale face on cold paper; Mr Morse had recently announced a way of transmitting messages down metal wires.

Had you mentioned magic or Faerie to any of them, they would have smiled at you disdainfully, except, perhaps for

Mr Dickens, at the time a young man, and beardless. He would have looked at you wistfully.

People were coming to the British Isles that spring. They came in ones, and they came in twos, and they landed at Dover or in London or in Liverpool: men and women with skins as pale as paper, skins as dark as volcanic rock, skins the colour of cinnamon, speaking in a multitude of tongues. They arrived all through April, and they travelled by steam train, by horse, by caravan or cart, and many of them walked.

At that time Dunstan Thorn was eighteen, and he was not a romantic.

He had nut-brown hair, and nut-brown eyes, and nut-brown freckles. He was middling tall, and slow of speech. He had an easy smile, which illuminated his face from within, and he dreamed, when he daydreamed in his father's meadow, of leaving the village of Wall and all its unpredictable charm, and going to London, or Edinburgh, or Dublin, or some great town where nothing was dependent on which way the wind was blowing. He worked on his father's farm and owned nothing save a small cottage in a far field given to him by his parents.

Visitors were coming to Wall that April for the fair, and Dunstan resented them. Mr Bromios's inn, the *Seventh Magpie*, normally a warren of empty rooms, had filled a week earlier, and now the strangers had begun to take rooms in the farms and private houses, paying for their lodgings with strange coins, with herbs and spices, and even with gemstones.

As the day of the fair approached the atmosphere of anticipation mounted. People were waking earlier, counting days, counting minutes. The guards on the gate, at the sides of the wall, were restive and nervous. Figures and shadows moved in the trees at the edge of the meadow.

In the *Seventh Magpie*, Bridget Comfrey, who was widely regarded as the most beautiful pot-girl in living memory, was provoking friction between Tommy Forester, with whom she had been seen to step out over the previous year, and a huge man with dark eyes and a small, chittering monkey. The man spoke little English, but he smiled expressively whenever Bridget came by.

In the pub's taproom the regulars sat in awkward proximity to the visitors, speaking so:

'It's only every nine years.'

'They say in the old days it was every year, at mid-summer.'

'Ask Mister Bromios. He'll know.'

Mr Bromios was tall, and his skin was olive; his black hair was curled tightly on his head; his eyes were green. As the girls of the village became women they took notice of Mr Bromios, but he did not return their notice. It was said he had come to the village quite some time ago, a visitor. But he had stayed in the village; and his wine was good, so the locals agreed.

A loud argument broke out in the public lounge between Tommy Forester and the dark-eyed man, whose name appeared to be Alum Bey.

'Stop them! In the name of Heaven! Stop them!' shouted Bridget. 'They're going out the back to fight over me!' And she tossed her head, prettily, so that the light of the oil lamps caught her perfect golden curls.

Nobody moved to stop the men, although a number of people, villagers and newcomers alike, went outside to spectate.

Tommy Forester removed his shirt and raised his fists in front of him. The stranger laughed, and spat on the grass, and then he seized Tommy's right hand and sent him flying onto the ground, chin-first. Tommy clambered to his feet and ran at the stranger. He landed a glancing blow on the man's cheek, before finding himself face-down in the dirt, his face being slammed into the mud, with the wind knocked out of him. Alum Bey sat on top of him and chuckled, and said something in Arabic.

That quickly, and that easily, the fight was over.

Alum Bey climbed off Tommy Forester and he strutted over to Bridget Comfrey, bowed low to her, and grinned with gleaming teeth.

Bridget ignored him, and ran to Tommy. 'Why, whatever has he done to you, my sweet?' she asked, and mopped the mud from his face with her apron and called him all manner of endearments.

Alum Bey went, with the spectators, back into the public rooms of the inn, and he graciously bought Tommy Forester a bottle of Mr Bromios's Chablis when Tommy returned. Neither of them was quite certain who had won, who had lost.

Dunstan Thorn was not in the *Seventh Magpie* that evening: he was a practical lad, who had, for the last six months, been courting Daisy Hempstock, a young woman of similar practicality. They would walk, on fair evenings, around the village, and discuss the theory of crop rotation, and the weather, and other such sensible matters; and on these walks, upon which they were invariably accompanied by Daisy's mother and younger sister walking a healthy six paces behind, they would, from time to time, stare at each other lovingly.

At the door to the Hempstocks' Dunstan would pause, and bow, and take his farewell.

And Daisy Hempstock would walk into her house, and remove her bonnet, and say, 'I *do* so wish Mister Thorn would make up his mind to propose. I am sure Papa would not be averse to it.'

'Indeed, I am sure that he would not,' said Daisy's mama on this evening, as she said on every such evening, and she removed her own bonnet and her gloves and led her daughters to the drawing room, in which a very tall gentleman with a very long black beard was sitting, sorting through his pack. Daisy, and her mama, and her sister, bobbed curtseys to the gentleman (who spoke little English, and had arrived a few days before). The temporary lodger, in his turn, stood and bowed to them, then returned to his pack of wooden oddments, sorting, arranging and polishing.

***

It was chilly that April, with the awkward changeability of English spring.

The visitors came up the narrow road through the forest from the south; they filled the spare-rooms, they bunked out in cow byres and barns. Some of them raised coloured tents, some of them arrived in their own caravans drawn by huge grey horses or by small, shaggy ponies.

In the forest there was a carpet of bluebells.

On the morning of April the 29th Dunstan Thorn drew guard duty on the gap in the wall, with Tommy Forester. They stood on each side of the gap in the wall, and they waited.

Dunstan had done guard duty many times before, but hitherto his task had consisted of simply standing, and, on occasion, shooing away children.

Today he felt important: he held a wooden cudgel, and as each stranger to the village came up to the break in the wall, Dunstan or Tommy would say 'Tomorrow, tomorrow. No one's coming through today, good sirs.'

And the strangers would retreat a little way, and stare through the break in the wall at the unassuming meadow beyond it, at the unexceptional trees that dotted the meadow, at the rather dull forest behind it. Some of them attempted to strike up conversations with Dunstan or Tommy, but the young men, proud of their status as guards, declined to converse, contenting themselves by raising their heads, tightening their lips, and generally looking important.

At lunchtime, Daisy Hempstock brought by a small pot of shepherd's pie for them both, and Bridget Comfrey brought them each a mug of spiced ale.

And, at twilight, another two able-bodied young men of the village arrived to relieve them, carrying a lantern each, and Tommy and Dunstan walked down to the inn where Mr Bromios gave each of them a mug of his best ale – and his best ale was very fine indeed – as their reward for doing guard duty. There was a buzz of excitement in the inn, now crowded beyond believing. It was filled with visitors to the village from every nation in the world, or so it seemed to Dunstan who had no sense of distance beyond the woods that surrounded the village of Wall, so he regarded the tall gentleman in the black top hat at the table beside him, all the way up from London, with as much awe as he regarded the taller ebony-coloured gentleman in the white one-piece robe with whom he was dining.

Dunstan knew that it was rude to stare, and that, as a villager of Wall, he had every right to feel superior to all of the 'furriners.' But he could smell unfamiliar spices on the air, and hear men and women speaking to each other in a hundred tongues, and he gawked and gazed unashamedly.

The man in the black silk top hat noticed that Dunstan was staring at him, and motioned the lad over to him. 'D'you like treacle pudden'?' he asked abruptly, by way of introduction. 'Mutanabbi was called away, and there's more pudden' here than a man can manage on his own.'

Dunstan nodded. The treacle pudding was steaming invitingly on its plate.

'Well then,' said his new friend, 'help yourself.' He passed Dunstan a clean china bowl and a spoon. Dunstan needed no further encouragement, and he began to demolish the pudding.

'Now, young 'un,' said the tall gentleman in the black silk top hat to Dunstan, once their bowls and the pudding-plate were quite empty, 'it'd seem the inn has no more rooms; also that every room in the village has already been let.'

'Is that so?' said Dunstan, unsurprised.

'That it is,' said the gentleman in the top hat. 'And what I was wondering was, would you know of a house that might have a room?'

Dunstan shrugged. 'All the rooms have gone by now,' he said. 'I remember that when I was a boy of nine, my mother and my father sent me to sleep out in the rafters of the cow byre for a week, and let my room to a lady from the Orient, and her family and servants. She left me a kite, as a thank you, and I flew it from the meadow until one day it snapped its string and flew away into the sky.'

'Where do you live now?' asked the gentleman in the top hat.

'I have a cottage on the edge of my father's land,' Dunstan replied. 'It was our shepherd's cottage, until he died, two years ago last lammas-tide, and my parents gave it to me.'

'Take me to it,' said the gentleman in the hat, and it did not occur to Dunstan to refuse him.

The spring moon was high and bright, and the night was clear. They walked down from the village to the forest beneath it, and they walked the whole way past the Thorn family farm (where the gentleman in the top hat was startled by a cow, sleeping in the meadow, which snorted as it dreamed) until they reached Dunstan's cottage.

It had one room and a fireplace. The stranger nodded. 'I like this well enough,' he said. 'Come, Dunstan Thorn, I'll rent it from you for the next three days.'

'What'll you give me for it?'

'A golden sovereign, a silver sixpence, a copper penny, and a fresh shiny farthing,' said the man.

Now a golden sovereign for two nights was more than a fair rent, in the days when a farm-worker might hope to make fifteen pounds in a good year. Still, Dunstan hesitated. 'If you're here for the market,' he told the tall man, 'then it's miracles and wonders you'll be trading.'

The tall man nodded. 'So, it would be miracles and wonders that you would be after, is it?' He looked around Dunstan's one-room cottage again. It began to rain then, a gentle pattering on the thatch above them.

'Oh, very well,' said the tall gentleman, a trifle testily, 'a miracle, a wonder. Tomorrow, you shall attain your Heart's Desire. Now, here is your money,' and he took it from Dunstan's ear, with one easy gesture. Dunstan touched it to the iron nail on the cottage door, checking for faerie gold, then he bowed low to the gentleman, and walked off into the rain. He tied the money up in his handkerchief.

Dunstan walked to the cow byre in the pelting rain. He climbed into the hayloft and was soon asleep.

He was aware, in the night, of thunder and of lightning, although he did not wake; and then in the small hours of the morning he was woken by someone treading, awkwardly, on his feet.

'Sorry,' said a voice. 'That is to say, 'scuse me.'

'Who's that? Who's there?' said Dunstan.

'Just me,' said the voice. 'I'm here for the market. I was sleeping in a hollow tree for the night, but the lightnin' toppled it, cracked it like an egg it did and smashed it like a twig, and the rain got down my neck, and it threatened to get into my baggage, and there's things in there must be kept dry as dust, and I'd kept it safe as houses on all my travellings here, though it was wet as . . .'

'Water?' suggested Dunstan.

'Ever-so,' continued the voice in the darkness. 'So I was wonderin',' it continued, 'if you'd mind me stayin' here under your roof as I'm not very big, and I'd not disturb you or nothing.'

'Just don't tread on me,' sighed Dunstan.

It was then that a flash of lightning illuminated the byre, and in the light, Dunstan saw something small and hairy in the corner, wearing a large floppy hat. And then, darkness.

'I hope I'm not disturbin' you,' said the voice, which certainly sounded rather hairy, now Dunstan thought about it.

'You aren't,' said Dunstan, who was very tired.

'That's good,' said the hairy voice, 'because I wouldn't want to disturb you.'

'Please,' begged Dunstan, 'let me sleep. *Please*.'

There was a snuffling noise, which was replaced by a gentle snoring.

Dunstan rolled over in the hay. The person, whoever, whatever it was, farted, scratched itself, and began to snore once more.

Dunstan listened to the rain on the byre roof, and thought about Daisy Hempstock, and in his thoughts they were walking together, and six steps behind them walked a tall man with a top hat and a small, furry creature whose face Dunstan could not see. They were off to see his Heart's Desire . . .

***

There was bright sunlight on his face, and the cow byre was empty. He washed his face, and walked up to the farmhouse.

He put on his very best jacket, and his very best shirt, and his very best britches. He scraped the mud from his boots with his pocketknife. Then he walked into the farm kitchen, and kissed his mother on the cheek, and helped himself to a cottage loaf and a large pat of fresh-churned butter.

And then, with his money tied up in his fine Sunday cambric handkerchief, he walked up to the village of Wall and bade good morning to the guards on the gate.

Through the gap in the wall he could see coloured tents being raised, stalls being erected, coloured flags, and people walking back and forth.

'We're not to let anyone through until midday,' said the guard.

Dunstan shrugged, and went to the pub, where he pondered what he would buy with his savings (the shiny half-crown he had saved, and the lucky sixpence, with a hole drilled through it, on a leather thong around his neck) and with the additional pocket handkerchief filled with coins. He had, for the moment, quite forgotten there had been anything else promised the night before. At the stroke of midday Dunstan strode up to the wall and, nervously, as if he were breaking the greatest of taboos, he walked through beside, as he realized, the gentleman in the black silk top hat, who nodded to him.

'Ah. My landlord. And how are you today, sir?'

'Very well,' said Dunstan.

'Walk with me,' said the tall man. 'Let us walk together.'

They walked across the meadow, toward the tents.

'Have you been here before?' asked the tall man.

'I went to the last market, nine years ago. I was only a boy,' admitted Dunstan.

'Well,' said his tenant, 'remember to be polite, and take no gifts. Remember that you're a guest. And now, I shall give you the last part of the rent that I owe you. For I swore an oath. And my gifts last a long time. You and your firstborn child and his or her firstborn child . . . It's a gift that will last as long as I live.'

'And what would that be, sir?'

'Your Heart's Desire, remember,' said the gentleman in the top hat. 'Your Heart's Desire.'

Dunstan bowed, and they walked on toward the fair.

'Eyes, eyes! New eyes for old!' shouted a tiny woman in front of a table covered with bottles and jars filled with eyes of every kind and colour.

'Instruments of music from a hundred lands!'

'Penny whistles! Tuppenny hums! Threepenny choral anthems!'

'Try your luck! Step right up! Answer a simple riddle and win a wind-flower!'

'Everlasting lavender! Bluebell cloth!'

'Bottled dreams, a shilling a bottle!'

'Coats of night! Coats of twilight! Coats of dusk!'

'Swords of fortune! Wands of power! Rings of eternity!

Cards of grace! Roll-up, roll-up, step this way!'

'Salves and ointments, philtres and nostrums!'

Dunstan paused in front of a stall covered with tiny crystal ornaments; he examined the miniature animals, pondering getting one for Daisy Hempstock. He picked up a crystal cat, no bigger than his thumb. Sagely it blinked at him, and he dropped it, shocked; it righted itself in midair and, like a real cat, fell on its four paws. Then it stalked over to the corner of the stall and began to wash itself.

Dunstan walked on, through the thronged market.

It was bustling with people; all the strangers who had come to Wall in the previous weeks were there, and many of the inhabitants of the town of Wall as well. Mr Bromios had set up a wine-tent and was selling wines and pasties to the village folk, who were often tempted by the foods being sold by the folk from Beyond the Wall but had been told by their grandparents, who had got it from *their* grandparents, that it was deeply, utterly wrong to eat fairy food, to eat fairy fruit, to drink fairy water and sip fairy wine.

For every nine years, the folk from Beyond the Wall and over the hill set up their stalls, and for a day and a night the meadow played host to the Faerie Market; and there was, for one day and one night in nine years, commerce between the nations.

There were wonders for sale, and marvels, and miracles; there were things undreamed-of and objects unimagined (*what need*, Dunstan wondered, *could someone have of the storm-filled eggshells?*). He jingled his money in his pocket handkerchief, and looked for something small and inexpensive with which to amuse Daisy.

He heard a gentle chiming in the air, above the hubbub of the market; and this he walked toward.

He passed a stall in which five huge men were dancing to the music of a lugubrious hurdy-gurdy being played by a mournful-looking black bear; he passed a stall where a balding man in a brightly coloured kimono was smashing

china plates and tossing them into a burning bowl from
which coloured smoke was pouring, all the while calling out
to the passersby.

The chinkling chiming grew louder.

Reaching the stall from which the sound was emanating,
he saw that it was deserted. It was festooned with flowers:
blue-bells and foxgloves and harebells and daffodils, but also
with violets and lilies, with tiny crimson dog-roses, pale
snowdrops, blue forget-me-nots and a profusion of other
flowers Dunstan could not name. Each flower was made of
glass or crystal, spun or carved, he could not tell: they
counterfeited life perfectly. And they chimed and jingled like
distant glass bells.

'Hello?' called Dunstan.

'Good morrow to you, on this Market Day,' said the stall
holder, clambering down from the painted caravan parked
behind the stall, and she smiled widely at him with white
teeth in a dusky face. She was one of the folk from Beyond
the Wall, he could tell at once from her eyes, and her ears
which were visible beneath her curly black hair. Her eyes
were a deep violet, while her ears were the ears of a cat,
perhaps, gently curved, and dusted with a fine, dark fur. She
was quite beautiful.

Dunstan picked up a flower from the stall. 'It's very lovely,'
he said. It was a violet, and it chinkled and sang as he held
it, making a noise similar to that produced by wetting a
finger and rubbing it, gently, around a wineglass. 'How much
is it?'

She shrugged, and a delightful shrug it was.

'The cost is never discussed at the outset,' she told him.
'It might be a great deal more than you are prepared to pay;
and then you would leave, and we would both be the poorer
for it. Let us discuss the merchandise in a more general
way.'

Dunstan paused. It was then that the gentleman with the
black silk top hat passed by the stall. 'There,' murmured

Dunstan's lodger. 'My debt to you is settled, and my rent is paid in full.'

Dunstan shook his head as if to clear it of a dream, and turned back to the young lady. 'So where do these flowers come from?' he asked.

She smiled knowingly. 'On the side of Mount Calamon a grove of glass flowers grows. The journey there is perilous, and the journey back is more so.'

'And of what purpose are they?' asked Dunstan.

'The use and function of these flowers is chiefly decorative and recreational; they bring pleasure; they can be given to a loved one as a token of admiration and affection, and the sound they make is pleasing to the ear. Also, they catch the light most delightfully.' She held a bluebell up to the light; and Dunstan could not but observe that the colour of sunlight glittering through the purple crystal was inferior in both hue and shade to that of her eyes.

'I see,' said Dunstan.

'They are also used in certain spells and cantrips. If sir is a magician . . .?'

Dunstan shook his head. There was, he noticed, something remarkable about the young lady.

'Ah. Even so, they are delightful things,' she said, and smiled again.

The remarkable thing was a thin silver chain that ran from the young lady's wrist, down to her ankle and into the painted caravan behind her.

Dunstan remarked upon it.

'The chain? It binds me to the stall. I am the personal slave of the witch-woman who owns the stall. She caught me many years ago – as I played by the waterfalls in my father's lands, high in the mountains – luring me on and on in the form of a pretty frog always but a moment out of my reach, until I had left my father's lands, unwittingly, whereupon she resumed her true shape and popped me into a sack.'

'And you are her slave forever?'

'Not forever,' and at that the faerie girl smiled. 'I gain my freedom on the day the moon loses her daughter, if that occurs in a week when two Mondays come together. I await it with patience. And in the meantime I do as I am bid, and also I dream. Will you buy a flower from me now, young master?'

'My name is Dunstan.'

'And an honest name it is, too,' she said with a teasing grin. 'Where are your pincers, Master Dunstan? Will you catch the devil by the nose?'

'And what is your name?' asked Dunstan, blushing a deep red.

'I no longer have a name. I am a slave, and the name I had was taken from me. I answer to "hey, you!" or to "girl!" or to "foolish slattern!" or to many another imprecation.'

Dunstan noticed how the silken fabric of her robe pressed itself against her body; he was aware of elegant curves, and of her violet eyes upon him, and he swallowed.

Dunstan put his hand in his pocket and pulled out his kerchief. He could no longer look at the woman. He tumbled out his money onto the counter. 'Take enough for this,' he said, picking a pure white snowdrop from the table.

'We do not take money at this stall.' She pushed the coins back toward him.

'No? What will you take?' For by now he was quite agitated, and his only mission was to obtain a flower for . . . for Daisy, Daisy Hempstock . . . to obtain his flower and to depart, for, truth to tell, the young lady was making him exceedingly uncomfortable.

'I could take the colour of your hair,' she said, 'or all of your memories before you were three years of age. I could take the hearing from your left ear – not all of it, just enough that you'd not enjoy music or appreciate the running of a river or the soughing of the wind.'

Dunstan shook his head.

'Or a kiss from you. One kiss, here on my cheek.'

'That I'll pay with goodwill!' said Dunstan, and with that he leaned across the stall, amid the twinkling jingling of the crystal flowers, and planted a chaste kiss on her soft cheek. He smelled the scent of her then, intoxicating, magical; it filled the front of his head and his chest and his mind.

'There, now,' she said, and she passed him his snowdrop. He took it with hands that suddenly seemed to him to be huge and clumsy and not at all small and in every way perfect like the hands of the faerie girl. 'And I'll see you back here tonight, Dunstan Thorn, when the moon goes down. Come here and hoot like a little owl. Can you do that?'

He nodded, and stumbled away from her; he did not need to ask how she knew his surname; she had taken it from him along with certain other things, such as his heart, when he had kissed her.

The snowdrop chimed in his hand.

***

'Why, Dunstan Thorn,' said Daisy Hempstock, when he encountered her by Mr Bromios's tent, sitting with her family and Dunstan's parents, eating great brown sausages and drinking porter, 'whatever is the matter?'

'I brought you a gift,' Dunstan muttered, and thrust the chiming snowdrop toward her; it glinted in the afternoon sunlight. She took it from him, puzzled, with fingers still shiny with sausage grease. Impulsively, Dunstan leaned forward and, in front of her mother and father and sister, in front of Bridget Comfrey and Mr Bromios and all, he kissed her on her fair cheek.

The outcry was predictable; but Mr Hempstock, who had not lived on the border of Faerie and the Lands Beyond for fifty-seven years for nothing, exclaimed, 'Hush, now! Look at his eyes. Can't you see the poor boy's dazed in his wits, dazed and confused? He's bespelled, I'll wager you. Hoy! Tommy Forester! Come here; take young Dunstan Thorn back to the village and keep an eye on him; let him sleep if he wishes, or talk if it's talk he needs . . .'

Tommy walked Dunstan out of the market and back to the village of Wall.

'There, now, Daisy,' said her mother, stroking her hair, 'he's just a little elf-touched, that's all. No need to take on so.' And she pulled a lace kerchief from her capacious bosom, and dabbed at her daughter's cheeks, which had suddenly become covered with tears.

Daisy looked up at her, and seized the handkerchief, and blew her nose upon it, and sniffled into it. And Mrs Hempstock observed, with a certain perplexity, that Daisy appeared to be smiling through her tears.

'But Mother, Dunstan *kissed* me,' said Daisy Hempstock, and she fixed the crystal snowdrop at the front of her bonnet, where it chimed and glistened.

After some time spent searching for it, Mr Hempstock and Dunstan's father found the stall where the crystal flowers were being sold; but the stall was being run by an elderly woman, accompanied by an exotic and very beautiful bird, which was chained to its perch by a thin silver chain. There was no reasoning with the old woman, for when they tried to question her about what had happened to Dunstan, all her talk was of one of the prizes of her collection, given away by a good-for-nothing, and that was what came of ingratitude, and of these sad modern times, and of today's servants.

***

In the empty village (for who'd be in the village during the Faerie Market?), Dunstan was taken into the *Seventh Magpie*, and given a wooden settle on which to sit. He rested his forehead on his hand, and stared off into no-one-knows-where and, from time to time, sighed huge sighs, like the wind.

Tommy Forester tried to talk to him, saying 'Now then, old

fellow, buck up, that's the ticket, let's see a smile, eh? How's about something to eat then? Or something to drink? No? My word, you do look queer, Dunstan, old fellow . . .' but gaining no response of any kind, Tommy began to pine after the market himself, where even now (he rubbed his tender jaw) the lovely Bridget was undoubtedly being escorted by some huge and imposing gentleman with exotic clothes and a little monkey that chattered. And, having assured himself that his friend would be safe in the empty inn, Tommy walked back through the village to the gap in the wall.

As Tommy reentered the market, he observed that the place was a hubbub: a wild place of puppet shows, of jugglers and dancing animals, of horses for auction and all kinds of things for sale or barter.

Later, at twilight, a different kind of people came out. There was a crier, who cried news as a modern newspaper prints headlines – 'The Master of Stormhold Suffers a Mysterious Malady!', 'The Hill of Fire Has Moved to the Fastness of Dene!', 'The Squire of Garamond's Only Heir is Transformed into a Gruntling Pig-wiggin!' – and would for a coin expand further on these stories.

The sun set, and a huge spring moon appeared, high already in the heavens. A chill breeze blew. Now the traders retreated into their tents, and the visitors to the market found themselves whispered at, invited to partake of numerous wonders, each available for a price.

And as the moon came low on the horizon Dunstan Thorn walked quietly down the cobbled streets of the village of Wall. He passed many a merry-maker – visitor or foreigner – although few enough of them observed him as he walked.

He slipped through the gap in the wall – thick it was, the wall – and Dunstan found himself wondering, as his father had before him, what would happen were he to walk along the top of it.

Through the gap and into the meadow, and that night, for the first time in his life, Dunstan entertained thoughts of continuing on through the meadow, of crossing the stream and vanishing into the trees on its far side. He entertained these thoughts awkwardly, as a man entertains unexpected guests. Then, as he reached his objective, he pushed these thoughts away, as a man apologizes to his guests, and leaves them, muttering something about a prior engagement.

The moon was setting.

Dunstan raised his hands to his mouth and hooted. There was no response; the sky above was a deep colour – blue perhaps, or purple, not black – sprinkled with more stars than the mind could hold.

He hooted once more.

'That,' she said severely in his ear, 'is nothing like a little owl. A snowy owl it could be, a barn owl, even. If my ears were stopped up with twigs perhaps I'd imagine it an eagle-owl. But it's not a little owl.'

Dunstan shrugged, and grinned, a little foolishly. The faerie woman sat down beside him. She intoxicated him: he was breathing her, sensing her through the pores of his skin. She leaned close to him.

'Do you think you are under a spell, pretty Dunstan?'

'I do not know.'

She laughed, and the sound was a clear rill bubbling over rocks and stones.

'You are under no spell, pretty boy, pretty boy.' She lay back in the grass and stared up at the sky. 'Your stars,' she asked. 'What are they like?' Dunstan lay beside her in the cool grass, and stared up at the night sky. There was certainly something odd about the stars: perhaps there was more colour in them, for they glittered like tiny gems; perhaps there was something about the number of tiny stars, the constellations; something was strange and wonderful about the stars. But then . . .

They lay back to back, staring up at the sky.

'What do you want from life?' asked the faerie lass.

'I don't know,' he admitted. 'You, I think.'

'I want my freedom,' she said.

Dunstan reached down to the silver chain that ran from her wrist to her ankle, and off away in the grass. He tugged on it. It was stronger than it looked.

'It was fashioned of cat's breath and fish-scales and moon-light mixed in with the silver,' she told him. 'Unbreakable until the terms of the spell are concluded.'

'Oh.' He moved back onto the grass.

'I should not mind it, for it is a long, long chain; but the knowledge of it irks me, and I miss my father's land. And the witch-woman is not the best of mistresses . . .'

And she was quiet. Dunstan leaned over toward her, reached a hand up to her face, felt something wet and hot splash against his hand.

'Why, you are crying.'

She said nothing. Dunstan pulled her toward him, wiping ineffectually at her face with his big hand; and then he leaned into her sobbing face and, tentatively, uncertain of whether or not he was doing the correct thing given the circumstances, he kissed her, full upon her burning lips.

There was a moment of hesitation, and then her mouth opened against his, and her tongue slid into his mouth, and he was, under the strange stars, utterly, irrevocably, lost.

He had kissed before, with the girls of the village, but he had gone no further.

His hand felt her small breasts through the silk of her dress, touched the hard nubs of her nipples. She clung to him, hard, as if she were drowning, fumbling with his shirt, with his britches.

She was so small; he was scared he would hurt her and break her. He did not. She wriggled and writhed beneath him, gasping and kicking, and guiding him with her hand.

She placed a hundred burning kisses on his face and chest, and then she was above him, straddling him, gasping and laughing, sweating and slippery as a minnow, and he was arching and pushing and exulting, his head full of her and only her, and had he known her name he would have called it out aloud.

At the end, he would have pulled out, but she held him inside her, wrapped her legs around him, pushed against him so hard that he felt that the two of them occupied the same place in the universe. As if, for one powerful, engulfing moment, they were the same person, giving and receiving, as the stars faded into the predawn sky.

They lay together, side by side.

The faerie woman adjusted her silk robe and was once more decorously covered. Dunstan pulled his britches back up, with regret. He squeezed her small hand in his.

The sweat dried on his skin, and he felt chilled and lonely. He could see her now, as the sky lightened into a dawn grey. Around them animals were stirring: horses stamped, birds began, waking, to sing the dawn in, and, here and there across the market meadow, those in the tents were beginning to rise and move. 'Now, get along with you,' she said softly, and looked at him, half regretfully, with eyes as violet as the cirrus clouds, high in the dawn sky. And she kissed him, gently, on the mouth, with lips that tasted of crushed blackberries, then she stood up and walked back into the gypsy caravan behind the stall.

Dazed and alone, Dunstan walked through the market, feeling a great deal older than his eighteen years.

He returned to the cow byre, took off his boots, and slept until he woke, when the sun was high in the sky.

On the following day the market finished, although Dunstan did not return to it, and the foreigners left the village and life in Wall returned to normal, which was perhaps slightly less normal than life in most villages (particularly when the wind was in the wrong direction) but was, all things considered, normal enough.

***

Two weeks after the market, Tommy Forester proposed marriage to Bridget Comfrey, and she accepted. And the week after that, Mrs Hempstock came to visit Mrs Thorn of a morning. They took tea in the parlour.

'It is a blessing about the Forester boy,' said Mrs Hempstock.

'That it is,' said Mrs Thorn. 'Have another scone, my dear. I expect your Daisy shall be a bridesmaid.'

'I trust she shall,' said Mrs Hempstock, '*if* she should live so long.'

Mrs Thorn looked up, alarmed. 'Why, she is not ill, Mrs Hempstock? Say it is not so.'

'She does not eat, Mrs Thorn. She wastes away. She drinks a little water from time to time.'

'Oh, my!'

Mrs Hempstock went on, 'Last night I finally discovered the cause. It is your Dunstan.'

'Dunstan? He has not . . .' Mrs Thorn raised one hand to her mouth.

'Oh, no,' said Mrs Hempstock, hastily shaking her head and pursing her lips, 'nothing like that. He has ignored her. She has not seen him for days and days. She has taken it into her head that he no longer cares for her, and all she does is hold the snowdrop he gave her, and she sobs.'

Mrs Thorn measured out more tea from the jar into the pot, added hot water. 'Truth to tell,' she admitted, 'we're a little concerned about Dunstan, Thorney and me. He's been *mooning*. That's the only word for it. His work isn't getting done. Thorney was saying that he needs some settling down, that boy. If he'd but settle down, why Thorney was saying he'd settle all the Westward Meadows on the lad.'

Mrs Hempstock nodded slowly. 'Hempstock would certainly not be averse to seeing our Daisy happy. Certain he'd settle a flock of our sheep on the girl.' The Hempstocks' sheep were notoriously the finest for miles around: shaggy-coated and intelligent (for sheep), with curling horns and sharp hooves. Mrs Hempstock and Mrs Thorn sipped their tea. And so it was settled.

Dunstan Thorn was married in June to Daisy Hempstock. And if the groom seemed a little distracted, well, the bride was as glowing and lovely as ever any bride has been.

Behind them, their fathers discussed the plans for the farmhouse they would build for the newlyweds in the western meadow. Their mothers agreed how lovely Daisy looked, and what a pity it was that Dunstan had stopped Daisy from wearing the snowdrop he had bought for her at the market at the end of April, in her wedding dress.

And it is there we will leave them, in a falling flurry of rose petals, scarlet and yellow and pink and white.

Or almost.

They lived in Dunstan's cottage, while their little farmhouse was erected, and they were certainly happy enough; and the day-to-day business of raising sheep, and herding sheep, and shearing them, and nursing them, slowly took the faraway look from Dunstan's eyes.

First autumn came, then winter. It was at the end of February, in lambing season, when the world was cold, and a bitter wind howled down the moors and through the leafless forest, when icy rains fell from the leaden skies in continual drizzling showers, at six in the evening, after the sun had set and the sky was dark, that a wicker basket was pushed through the space in the wall. The guards, on each side of the gap, at first did not notice the basket. They were facing the wrong way, after all, and it was dark and wet, and they were busy stamping the ground and staring gloomily and longingly at the lights of the village.

And then a high, keening wail began.

It was then that they looked down, and saw the basket at their feet. There was a bundle in the basket: a bundle of oiled silk and woolen blankets, from the top of which protruded a red, bawling face, with screwed-up little eyes and a mouth, open and vocal, and hungry.

And there was, attached to the baby's blanket with a silver pin, a scrap of parchment, upon which was written in an elegant, if slightly archaic, handwriting the following words:

Tristran Thorn

Chapter Two

In Which Tristran Thorn Grows to Manhood and Makes a Rash Promise

Years passed.

The next Faerie Market was held on schedule on the other side of the wall. Young Tristran Thorn, eight years old, did not attend, finding himself packed off to stay with extremely distant relations in a village a day's ride away.

His little sister, Louisa, six months his junior, was, however, allowed to go to the market, and this was a source of great ranklement to the boy, as was the fact that Louisa brought back from the market a glass globe, filled with speckles of light that glittered and flashed in the twilight, and which cast a warm and gentle radiance into the darkness of their bedroom in the farmhouse, while all Tristran brought back from his relatives was a nasty case of the measles.

Shortly afterward, the farm cat had three kittens: two black-and-white ones like herself, and a tiny kitten with a dusty blue sheen to her coat, and eyes that changed colour depending on her mood, from green and gold to salmon, scarlet and vermilion.

This kitten was given to Tristran to make up for missing
the market. She grew slowly, the blue cat, and she was the
sweetest cat in the world, until, one evening, she began to
prowl the house impatiently, to *mrowll* and to flash her eyes,
which were the purple-red of foxgloves; and when Tristran's
father came back from a day in the fields, the cat yowled,
bolted through the door and was off into the dusk.

The guards on the wall were for people, not cats; and
Tristran, who was twelve by this time, never saw the blue cat
again. He was inconsolable for a while. His father came into
his bedroom one night and sat at the end of his bed, saying
gruffly, 'She'll be happier, over the wall. With her own kind.
Don't you fret now, lad.'

His mother said nothing to him about the matter, as she
said little to him on any subject. Sometimes Tristran would
look up to see his mother staring at him intently, as if she
were trying to tease some secret from his face.

Louisa, his sister, would needle him about this as they
walked to the village school in the morning, as she would
goad him about so many other things: the shape of his ears,
for example (the right ear was flat against his head, and
almost pointed; the left one was not), and about the foolish
things he said: once he told her that the tiny clouds, fluffy
and white, that clustered across the horizon at sunset as they
walked home from school, were sheep. It was no matter that
he later claimed that he had meant simply that they
reminded him of sheep, or that there was something fluffy
and sheeplike about them. Louisa laughed and teased and
goaded like a goblin; and what was worse, she told the other
children, and incited them to 'baa' quietly whenever Tristran
walked past. Louisa was a born inciter, and danced circles
around her brother.

The village school was a fine school, and under the
tutelage of Mrs Cherry the schoolmistress Tristran Thorn
learned all about fractions, and longitude and latitude; he
could ask in French for the pen of the gardener's aunt, indeed

for the pen of his own aunt; he learned the Kings and Queens of England from William the Conqueror, 1066, to Victoria, 1837. He learned his reading, and had a fair copperplate hand. Travellers to the village were rare, but occasionally a pedlar would come through the village, selling 'penny dreadful' accounts of grisly murders, fateful encounters, dire doings and remarkable escapes. Most pedlars sold song sheets, two for a penny, and families would buy them and gather about their pianos to sing songs such as 'Cherry Ripe' and 'In My Father's Garden.'

So the days went by, and the weeks went by, and the years went by also. At age fourteen, by a process of osmosis, of dirty jokes, whispered secrets and filthy ballads, Tristran learned of sex. When he was fifteen he hurt his arm falling from the apple tree outside Mr Thomas Forester's house: more specifically, from the apple tree outside Miss Victoria Forester's bedroom window. To Tristran's regret, he had caught no more than a pink and tantalizing glimpse of Victoria, who was his sister's age and, without any doubt, the most beautiful girl for a hundred miles around.

By the time Victoria was seventeen, and Tristran also, she was in all probability, he was certain, the most beautiful girl in the British Isles. Tristran would have insisted on the most beautiful girl in the entire British Empire, if not the world, and boxed you, or been prepared to, had you argued with him. You would have been hard-pressed to find anyone in Wall who would have argued with him, though; she turned many heads and, in all probability, broke many hearts.

A description: She had her mother's grey eyes and heart-shaped face, her father's curling chestnut hair. Her lips were red and perfectly shaped, her cheeks blushed prettily when she spoke. She was pale, and utterly delightful. When she was sixteen she had fought vigorously with her mother, for Victoria had taken it into her head that she would work in the *Seventh Magpie* as a pot-maid. 'I have spoken to Mister

Bromios about this,' she told her mother, 'and *he* has no objection.'

'What Mister Bromios thinks or does not think,' replied her mother, the former Bridget Comfrey 'is neither here nor there. That is a most improper occupation for a young lady.'

The village of Wall watched the battle of wills with fascination, wondering what the outcome would be, for no one crossed Bridget Forester: she had a tongue that could, the villagers said, blister the paint from a barn door and tear the bark from an oak. There was no one in the village who would have wanted to get on the wrong side of Bridget Forester, and they did say that the wall would be more likely to walk than for Bridget Forester to change her mind.

Victoria Forester, however, was used to having her own way, and, if all else failed, or even if it did not, she would appeal to her father, and he would accede to her demands. But here even Victoria was surprised, for her father agreed with her mother, saying that working in the bar at the *Seventh Magpie* was something that a well-brought-up young lady would not do. And Thomas Forester set his chin and there the matter ended.

***

Every boy in the village was in love with Victoria Forester. And many a sedate gentleman, quietly married with grey in his beard, would stare at her as she walked down the street, becoming, for a few moments, a boy once more, in the spring of his years with a spring in his step.

'They say that Mister Monday himself is counted amongst your admirers,' said Louisa Thorn to Victoria Forester one afternoon in May, in the apple orchard.

Five girls sat beside, and upon the branches of, the oldest apple tree in the orchard, its huge trunk making a fine seat and support; and whenever the May breeze blew the pink blossoms tumbled down like snow, coming to rest in their hair and on their skirts. The afternoon sunlight dappled green and silver and gold through the leaves in the apple orchard.

'Mister Monday,' said Victoria Forester with disdain, 'is five and forty years of age if he is a day.' She made a face to indicate just how old five and forty is, when you happen to be seventeen.

'Anyway,' said Cecilia Hempstock, Louisa's cousin, 'he has already been married. I would not wish to marry someone who had already been married. It would be,' she opined, 'like having someone else break in one's own pony.'

'Personally I would imagine that to be the *sole* advantage of marrying a widower,' said Amelia Robinson. 'That someone else would have removed the rough edges; broken him in, if you will. Also, I would imagine that by that age his lusts would long since have been sated, and abated, which would free one from a number of indignities.'

A flurry of hastily suppressed giggles amid the apple blossom.

'Still,' said Lucy Pippin hesitantly, 'it would be nice to live in the big house, and to have a coach and four, and to be able to travel to London for the season, and to Bath to take the waters, or to Brighton for the sea-bathing, even if Mister Monday *is* five and forty.'

The other girls shrieked, and flung handfuls of apple blossom at her, and none shrieked more loudly, or flung more blossom, than Victoria Forester.

***

Tristran Thorn, at the age of seventeen, and only six months older than Victoria, was half the way between a boy and a man, and was equally uncomfortable in either role; he seemed to be composed chiefly of elbows and Adam's apples with a constellation of acne-spots across his right cheek. His hair was the brown of sodden straw, and it stuck out at awkward, seventeen-year-old angles, wet and comb it howsoever much he tried.

He was painfully shy, which, as is often the manner of the painfully shy, he overcompensated for by being too loud at the wrong times. Most days Tristran was content – or as content as a seventeen-year-old youth with his world ahead of him can ever be – and when he daydreamed in the fields, or at the tall desk at the back of Monday and Brown's, the village shop, he fancied himself riding the train all the way to London or to Liverpool, or taking a steamship across the grey Atlantic to America, and making his fortune there among the savages in the new lands.

But there were times when the wind blew from beyond the wall, bringing with it the smell of mint and thyme and redcurrants, and at those times there were strange colours seen in the flames in the fireplaces of the village. When that wind blew, the simplest of devices – from lucifer matches to lantern-slides – would no longer function.

And, at those times, Tristran Thorn's daydreams were strange, guilty fantasies, muddled and odd, of journeys through forests to rescue Princesses from palaces, dreams of knights and trolls and mermaids. And when these moods came upon him, he would slip out of the house, and lie upon the grass, and stare up at the stars.

Few of us now have seen the stars as folk saw them then – our cities and towns cast too much light into the night – but, from the village of Wall, the stars were laid out like worlds or like ideas, uncountable as the trees in a forest or the leaves on a tree. Tristran would stare into the darkness of the sky until he thought of nothing at all, and then he would go back to his bed, and sleep like a dead man.

He was a gangling creature of potential, a barrel of dynamite waiting for someone or something to light his fuse; but no one did, so on weekends and in the evenings he helped his father on the farm, and during the day he worked for Mr Brown, at Monday and Brown's, as a clerk.

Monday and Brown's was the village shop. While they kept a number of necessaries in stock, much of their business was conducted by means of lists: villagers would give Mr Brown a list of what they needed, from potted meats to sheep-dip, from fish-knives to chimney-tiles; a clerk at Monday and Brown's would compile a master list of everything requested, and then Mr Monday would take the master list, and a dray pulled by two huge shire horses, and he would set off for the nearest county town, and return in a handful of days with the dray loaded high with goods of all description.

It was a cold, blustery day in late October, of the kind that always seems about to rain but never actually does, and it was late in the afternoon. Victoria Forester walked into Monday and Brown's with a list, written in her mother's precise handwriting, and she rang the small bell on the counter for service.

She looked slightly disappointed to see Tristran Thorn appear from the back room. 'Good day, Miss Forester.'

She smiled a tight smile, and handed Tristran her list.

It read as follows:

$^1/_2$ lb of sago
10 cans of sardines
1 bottle of mushroom ketchup
5 lb of rice
1 tin of golden syrup
2 lb of currants
a bottle of cochineal
1 lb of barley sugar
1 shilling box of Rowntrees Elect Cocoa
3d tin of Oakey's knife polish
6d of Brunswick black
1 packet of Swinborne's Isinglass
1 bottle of furniture cream
1 basting ladle

a ninepenny gravy strainer
a set of kitchen steps

Tristran read it to himself, looking for something about which he could begin to talk: a conversational gambit of some kind – any kind.

He heard his voice saying, 'You'll be having rice pudding, then, I would imagine, Miss Forester.' As soon as he said it, he knew it had been the wrong thing to say. Victoria pursed her perfect lips, and blinked her grey eyes, and said, 'Yes, Tristran. We shall be having rice pudding.'

And then she smiled at him, and said, 'Mother says that rice pudding in sufficient quantity will help to stave off chills and colds and other autumnal ailments.'

'My mother,' Tristran confessed, 'has always sworn by tapioca pudding.'

He put the list on a spike. 'We can deliver most of the provisions tomorrow morning, and the rest of it will come back with Mister Monday, early next week.'

There was a gust of wind, then, so strong that it rattled the windows of the village, and whirled and spun the weathercocks until they could not tell north from west or south from east.

The fire that was burning in the grate of Monday and Brown's belched and twisted in a flurry of greens and scarlets, topped with a fizz of silver twinkles, of the kind one can make for oneself at the parlour fire with a handful of tossed iron filings.

The wind blew from Faerie and the East, and Tristran Thorn suddenly found inside himself a certain amount of courage he had not suspected that he had possessed. 'You know, Miss Forester, I get off in a few minutes,' he said. 'Perhaps I could walk you a little way home. It's not much out of my way.' And he waited, his heart in his mouth, while Victoria Forester's grey eyes stared at him, amused. After what seemed like a hundred years she said, 'Certainly.'

Tristran hurried into the parlour, and informed Mr Brown that he would be off now. And Mr Brown grunted in a not entirely ill-natured way, and told Tristran that when *he* was younger he'd not only had to stay late each night and shut up the shop, but that he had also had to sleep on the floor beneath the counter with only his coat for a pillow.

Tristran agreed that he was indeed a lucky young man, and he wished Mr Brown a good night, then he took his coat from the coat-stand and his new bowler hat from the hat-stand, and stepped out onto the cobblestones, where Victoria Forester waited for him.

The autumn twilight turned into deep and early night as they walked. Tristran could smell the distant winter on the air – a mixture of night-mist and crisp darkness and the tang of fallen leaves.

They took a winding lane up toward the Forester farm, and the crescent moon hung white in the sky and the stars burned in the darkness above them.

'Victoria,' said Tristran, after a while.

'Yes, Tristran,' said Victoria, who had been preoccupied for much of the walk.

'Would you think it forward of me to kiss you?' asked Tristran.

'Yes,' said Victoria bluntly and coldly. 'Very forward.'

'Ah,' said Tristran.

They walked up Dyties Hill, not speaking; at the top of the hill they turned, and saw beneath them the village of Wall, all gleaming candles and lamps glimmering through windows, warm yellow lights that beckoned and invited; and above them the lights of the myriad stars, which glittered and twinkled and blazed, chilly and distant and more numerous than the mind could encompass.

Tristran reached down his hand and took Victoria's small hand in his. She did not pull away.

'Did you see that?' asked Victoria, who was gazing out over the landscape.

'I saw nothing,' said Tristran. 'I was looking at you.'

Victoria smiled in the moonlight.

'You are the most lovely woman in all the world,' said Tristran, from the bottom of his heart.

'Get along with you,' said Victoria, but she said it gently.

'What did you see?' asked Tristran.

'A falling star,' said Victoria. 'I believe they are not at all uncommon at this time of year.'

'Vicky,' said Tristran. 'Will you kiss me?'

'No,' she said.

'You kissed me when we were younger. You kissed me beneath the pledge-Oak, on your fifteenth birthday. And you kissed me last May Day, behind your father's cowshed.'

'I was another person then,' she said. 'And I shall not kiss you, Tristran Thorn.'

'If you will not kiss me,' asked Tristran, 'will you marry me?'

There was silence on the hill. Only the rustle of the October wind. Then a tinkling sound: it was the sound of the most beautiful girl in the whole of the British Isles laughing with delight and amusement.

'Marry you?' she repeated, incredulously. 'And why ever should I marry you, Tristran Thorn? What could you give me?'

'Give you?' he said. 'I would go to India for you, Victoria Forester, and bring you the tusks of elephants, and pearls as big as your thumb, and rubies the size of wren's eggs.

'I would go to Africa, and bring you diamonds the size of cricket balls. I would find the source of the Nile, and name it after you.

'I would go to America – all the way to San Francisco, to the gold-fields, and I would not come back until I had your weight in gold. Then I would carry it back here, and lay it at your feet.

'I would travel to the distant northlands did you but say the word, and slay the mighty polar bears, and bring you back their hides.'

'I think you were doing quite well,' said Victoria Forester, 'until you got to the bit about slaying polar bears. Be that as it may, little shop-boy and farm-boy, I shall not kiss you; neither shall I marry you.'

Tristran's eyes blazed in the moonlight. 'I would travel to far Cathay for you, and bring you a huge junk I would capture from the king of the pirates, laden with jade and silk and opium.

'I would go to Australia, at the bottom of the world,' said Tristran, 'and bring you. Um.' He ransacked the penny dreadfuls in his head, trying to remember if any of their heroes had visited Australia. 'A kangaroo,' he said. 'And opals,' he added. He was fairly sure about the opals.

Victoria Forester squeezed his hand. 'And whatever would I do with a kangaroo?' she asked. 'Now, we should be getting along, or my father and mother will be wondering what has kept me, and they will leap to some entirely unjustified conclusions. For I have not kissed you, Tristran Thorn.'

'Kiss me,' he pleaded. 'There is nothing I would not do for your kiss, no mountain I would not scale, no river I would not ford, no desert I would not cross.'

He gestured widely, indicating the village of Wall below them, the night sky above them. In the constellation of Orion, low on the Eastern horizon, a star flashed and glittered and fell.

'For a kiss, and the pledge of your hand,' said Tristran, grandiloquently, 'I would bring you that fallen star.'

He shivered. His coat was thin, and it was obvious he would not get his kiss, which he found puzzling. The manly heroes of the penny dreadfuls and shilling novels never had these problems getting kissed.

'Go on, then,' said Victoria. 'And if you do, I will.'

'What?' said Tristran.

'If you bring me that star,' said Victoria, 'the one that just fell, not another star, then I'll kiss you. Who knows what else

I might do. There: now you need not go to Australia, nor to
Africa, nor to far Cathay.'

'What?' said Tristran.

And Victoria laughed at him, then, and took back her
hand, and began to walk down the hill towards her father's
farm.

Tristran ran to catch her up. 'Do you mean it?' he asked
her.

'I mean it as much as you mean all your fancy words of
rubies and gold and opium,' she replied. 'What *is* an
opium?'

'Something in cough mixture,' said Tristran. 'Like
eucalyptus.'

'It does not sound particularly romantic,' said Victoria
Forester. 'Anyway, should you not be running off to retrieve
my fallen star? It fell to the East, over there.' And she
laughed again. 'Silly shop-boy. It is all you can do to ensure
that we have the ingredients for rice pudding.'

'And if I brought you the fallen star?' asked Tristran lightly.
'What would you give me? A kiss? Your hand in marriage?'

'Anything you desire,' said Victoria, amused.

'You swear it?' asked Tristran.

They were walking the last hundred yards now, up to the
Foresters' farmhouse. The windows burned with lamplight,
yellow and orange.

'Of course,' said Victoria, smiling.

The track to the Foresters' farm was bare mud, trodden
into mire by the feet of horses and cows and sheep and dogs.
Tristran Thorn went down on his knees in the mud, heedless
of his coat or his woolen trousers. 'Very well,' he said.

The wind blew from the east, then.

'I shall leave you here, my lady,' said Tristran Thorn. 'For
I have urgent business, to the East.' He stood up, unmindful
of the mud and mire clinging to his knees and coat, and he
bowed to her, and then he doffed his bowler hat.

Victoria Forester laughed at the skinny shop-boy, laughed

long and loud and delightfully, and her tinkling laughter followed him back down the hill, and away.

***

Tristran Thorn ran all the way home. Brambles snagged at his clothes as he ran and a branch knocked his hat from his head.

He stumbled, breathless and torn, into the kitchen of the house on Westward Meadows.

'Look at the state of you!' said his mother. 'Indeed! I never did!'

Tristran merely smiled at her.

'Tristran?' asked his father, who at five and thirty was still middling tall and still freckled, although there were more than a few silvering hairs in his nut-brown curls. 'Your mother spoke to you. Did you not hear her?'

'I beg your pardon, Father, Mother,' said Tristran, 'but I shall be leaving the village tonight. I may be gone for some time.'

'Foolishness and silliness!' said Daisy Thorn. 'I never heard such nonsense.'

But Dunstan Thorn saw the look in his son's eyes. 'Let me talk to him,' he said to his wife. She looked at him sharply, then she nodded. 'Very well,' she said. 'But who's going to sew up the boy's coat? That's what I would like to know.' She bustled out of the kitchen.

The kitchen fire fizzed in silver and glimmered green and violet. 'Where are you going?' asked Dunstan.

'East,' said his son.

East. His father nodded. There were two easts – east to the next country, through the forest, and East, the other side of the wall. Dunstan Thorn knew without asking to which his son was referring.

'And will you be coming back?' asked his father.

Tristran grinned widely. 'Of course,' he said.

'Well,' said his father. 'That's all right, then.' He scratched his nose. 'Have you given any thought to getting through the wall?'

Tristran shook his head. 'I'm sure I can find a way,' he said. 'If necessary, I'll fight my way past the guards.'

His father sniffed. 'You'll do no such thing,' he said. 'How would you like it if it was you was on duty, or me? I'll not see anyone hurt.' He scratched the side of his nose once more. 'Go and pack a bag, and kiss your mother good-bye, and I'll walk you down to the village.'

Tristran packed a bag, and his mother brought him six red, ripe apples and a cottage loaf and a round of white farmhouse cheese, which he placed inside his bag. Mrs Thorn would not look at Tristran. He kissed her cheek and bade her farewell. Then he walked into the village with his father.

Tristran had stood his first watch on the wall when he was sixteen years old. He had only been given one instruction: That it was the task of the guards to prevent anyone from coming through the gap in the wall from the village, by any means possible. If it was not possible to prevent them, then the guards must raise the village for help.

He wondered as they walked what his father had in mind. Perhaps the two of them together would overpower the guards. Perhaps his father would create some kind of distraction, and allow him to slip through . . . perhaps . . .

By the time they walked through the village and arrived at the gap in the wall, Tristran had imagined every possibility, except the one which occurred.

On wall duty that evening were Harold Crutchbeck and Mr Bromios. Harold Crutchbeck was a husky young man several years older than Tristran, the miller's son. Mr Bromios's hair was black, and curled, and his eyes were green, and his smile was white, and he smelled of grapes and of grape juice, of barley and of hops.

Dunstan Thorn walked up to Mr Bromios, and stood in

front of him. He stamped his feet against the evening chill.

'Evening, Mister Bromios. Evening, Harold,' said Dunstan.

'Evening, Mister Thorn,' said Harold Crutchbeck.

'Good evening, Dunstan,' said Mr Bromios. 'I trust you are well.'

Dunstan allowed as that he was; and they spoke of the weather, and agreed that it would be bad for the farmers, and that, from the quantity of holly berries and yew berries already apparent, it would be a cold, hard winter.

As he listened to them talking, Tristran was ready to burst with irritation and frustration, but he bit his tongue and said nothing.

Finally, his father said, 'Mister Bromios, Harold, I believe you both know my son Tristran?' Tristran raised his bowler hat to them, nervously.

And then his father said something he did not understand. 'I suppose you both know about where he came from,' said Dunstan Thorn.

Mr Bromios nodded, without speaking.

Harold Crutchbeck said he had heard tales, although you never should mind the half of what you hear.

'Well, it's true,' said Dunstan. 'And now it's time for him to go back.'

'There's a star . . .' Tristran began to explain, but his father hushed him to silence.

Mr Bromios rubbed his chin, and ran a hand through his thatch of black curls. 'Very well,' he said. He turned and spoke to Harold in a low voice, saying things Tristran could not hear.

His father pressed something cold into his hand.

'Go on with you, boy. Go, and bring back your star, and may God and all His angels go with you.'

And Mr Bromios and Harold Crutchbeck, the guards on the gate, stood aside to let him pass.

Tristran walked through the gap, with the stone wall on each side of him, into the meadow on the other side of the wall.

Turning, he looked back at the three men, framed in the gap, and wondered why they had allowed him through.

Then, his bag swinging in one hand, the object his father had pushed into his hand in the other, Tristran Thorn set off up the gentle hill, toward the woods.

***

As he walked, the chill of the night grew less, and once in the woods at the top of the hill Tristran was surprised to realize the moon was shining brightly down on him through a gap in the trees. He was surprised because the moon had set an hour before; and doubly surprised, because the moon that had set had been a slim, sharp silver crescent, and the moon that shone down on him now was a huge, golden harvest moon, full, and glowing, and deeply coloured.

The cold thing in his hand chimed once: a crystalline tinkling like the bells of a tiny glass cathedral. He opened his hand and held it up to the moonlight.

It was a snowdrop, made all of glass.

A warm wind stroked Tristran's face: it smelled like peppermint, and blackcurrant leaves, and red, ripe plums; and the enormity of what he had done descended on Tristran Thorn. He was walking into Faerie, in search of a fallen star, with no idea how he would find the star, nor how to keep himself safe and whole as he tried. He looked back and fancied that he could see the lights of Wall behind him, wavering and glimmering as if in a heat-haze, but still inviting.

And he knew that if he turned around and went back, no one would think any less of him for it – not his father, nor his mother; and even Victoria Forester would likely as not merely smile at him the next time she saw him, and call him 'shop-boy,' and add that stars, once fallen, often proved difficult in the finding.

He paused, then.

He thought of Victoria's lips, and her grey eyes, and the sound of her laughter. He straightened his shoulders, placed the crystal snowdrop in the top buttonhole of his coat, now undone. And, too ignorant to be scared, too young to be awed, Tristran Thorn passed beyond the fields we know . . . . . . and into Faerie.

Chapter Three

In Which We Encounter Several Other Persons, Many of Them Still Alive, With an Interest in the Fate of the Fallen Star

The Stormhold had been carved out of the peak of Mount Huon by the first lord of Stormhold, who reigned at the end of the First Age and into the beginning of the Second. It had been expanded, improved upon, excavated and tunnelled into by successive Masters of Stormhold, until the original mountain peak now raked the sky like the ornately carved tusk of some great, grey, granite beast. The Stormhold itself was perched high in the sky, where the thunder clouds gathered before they went down to the lower air, spilling rain and lightning and devastation upon the place beneath.

The eighty-first Lord of Stormhold lay dying in his chamber, which was carved from the highest peak like a hole in a rotten tooth. There is still death in the lands beyond the fields we know.

He summoned his children to his bedside and they came, the living and the dead of them, and they shivered in the cold granite halls. They gathered about his bed and waited respectfully, the living to his right side, the dead on his left.

Four of his sons were dead: Secundus, Quintus, Quartus and Sextus, and they stood unmoving, grey figures, insubstantial and silent.

Three of his sons remained alive: Primus, Tertius and Septimus. They stood, solidly, uncomfortably, on the right of the chamber, shifting from foot to foot, scratching their cheeks and noses, as if they were shamed by the silent repose of their dead brothers. They did not glance across the room toward their dead brothers, acting – as best they could – as if they and their father were the only ones in that cold room, where the windows were huge holes in the granite through which the cold winds blew. And whether this is because they could not see their dead brothers, or because, having murdered them (one apiece, save Septimus, who had killed both Quintus and Sextus, poisoning the former with a dish of spiced eels, and, rejecting artifice for efficiency and gravity, simply pushing Sextus off a precipice one night as they were admiring a lightning storm far below), they chose to ignore them, scared of guilt, or revelation, or ghosts, their father did not know.

Privately, the eighty-first lord had hoped that by the time his end came upon him, six of the seven young lords at Stormhold would be dead, and but one still alive. That one would be the eighty-second Lord of Stormhold and Master of the High Crags; it was, after all, how he had attained his own title several hundred years before.

But the youth of today were a pasty lot, with none of the get-up-and-go, none of the vigour and vim that he remembered from the days when he was young . . .

Somebody was saying something. He forced himself to concentrate.

'Father,' repeated Primus in his deep boom of a voice. 'We are all here. What would you do with us?'

The old man stared at him. With a ghastly wheezing he pulled a breath of the thin, chill air into his lungs, and then said, in high, cold tones, like the granite itself, 'I am dying. Soon my time will be done, and you will take my remains deep into the mountain, to the Hall of Ancestors, and you will place them – me – in the one-and-eightieth hollow you come to, which is to say, the first that is not occupied, and there you shall leave me. If you do not do this thing, you will each be cursed, and the tower of Stormhold shall tumble and fall.'

His three living sons said nothing. A murmur ran through the four dead sons, though: regret, perhaps, that their remains had been gobbled up by eagles, or carried away by the fast rivers, tumbled down waterfalls and off to the sea, never to rest in the Hall of Ancestors.

'Now. The matter of succession.' The lord's voice wheezed out of him, like the wind being squeezed from a pair of rotten bellows. His living sons raised their heads: Primus, the oldest, with white hairs in his thick brown beard, his nose aquiline, his eyes grey, looked expectant; Tertius, his beard red-and-golden, his eyes a tawny brown, looked wary; Septimus, his black beard still coming in, tall and crowlike, looked blank, as he always looked blank.

'Primus. Go to the window.'

Primus strode over to the opening in the rock wall and looked out.

'What do you see?'

'Nothing, sire. I see the evening sky above us, and clouds below us.'

The old man shivered beneath the mountain-bear skin that covered him.

'Tertius. Go to the window. What do you see?'

'Nothing, Father. It is as Primus told you. The evening sky hangs above us, the colour of a bruise, and clouds carpet the world beneath us, all grey and writhing.'

The old man's eyes twisted in his face like the mad eyes of a bird of prey. 'Septimus. You. Window.'

Septimus strolled to the window and stood beside,

although not too close to, his two elder brothers.

'And you? What do you see?'

He looked out of the opening. The wind was bitter on his face, and it made his eyes sting and tear. One star glimmered, faintly, in the indigo heavens.

'I see a star, Father.'

'Ahh,' wheezed the eighty-first lord. 'Bring me to the window.' His four dead sons looked at him sadly as his three living sons carried him to the window. The old man stood, or almost stood, leaning heavily on the broad shoulders of his children, staring into the leaden sky.

His fingers, swollen-knuckled and twiglike, fumbled with the topaz that hung on a heavy silver chain about his neck. The chain parted like a cobweb in the old man's grip. He held the topaz out in his fist, the broken ends of silver chain dangling.

The dead lords of Stormhold whispered amongst themselves, in the voices of the dead which sound like snow falling: the topaz was the Power of Stormhold. Who wore it would be Stormhold's master, as long as he was of the blood of Stormhold. To which of the surviving sons would the eighty-first lord give the stone?

The living sons said nothing, but looked, respectively, expectant, wary, and blank (but it was a deceptive blankness, the blankness of a rock face that one only realizes cannot be climbed when one is halfway up, and there is no longer any way down).

The old man pulled free of his sons, and stood straight and tall, then. He was, for a heartbeat, the lord of Stormhold who had defeated the Northern Goblins at the battle of Cragland's Head; who had fathered eight children, seven of them boys, on three wives; who had killed each of his four brothers in combat before he was twenty years old, although his oldest brother had been almost five times his age and a mighty warrior of great renown. It was this man who held up the topaz and said four words in a long-dead tongue, words which hung on the air like the strokes of a huge bronze gong.

Then he threw the stone into the air. The living brothers caught their breath, as the stone arced up over the clouds. It reached what they were certain must be the zenith of its curve, and then, defying all reason, it continued to rise into the air.

Other stars glittered in the night sky, now.

'To the one that retrieves the stone, which is the Power of Stormhold, I leave my blessing, and the Mastership of Stormhold and all its dominions,' said the eighty-first lord, his voice losing power as he spoke, until once again it was the creak of an old, old man, like the wind blowing through an abandoned house.

The brothers, living and dead, stared at the stone. It fell upwards into the sky until it was lost to sight.

'And should we capture eagles, and harness them, to drag us into the heavens?' asked Tertius, puzzled and annoyed.

His father said nothing. The last of the daylight faded, and the stars hung above them, uncountable in their glory.

One star fell.

Tertius thought, although he was not certain, that it was the first star of the evening, the one that his brother Septimus had remarked upon.

The star tumbled, a streak of light, through the night sky, and it tumbled down somewhere to the south and west of them.

'There,' whispered the eighty-first lord, and he fell to the stone floor of his chamber, and he breathed no more.

Primus scratched his beard, and looked down at the crumpled thing. 'I've half a mind,' he said, 'to push the old bastard's corpse out of the window. What was all that idiocy about?'

'Better not,' said Tertius. 'We don't want to see Stormhold tumble and fall. Nor do we want a curse on our heads, for that matter. Better just place him in the Hall of Ancestors.'

Primus picked his father's body up, and carried him back

to the furs of his bed. 'We will tell the people he is dead,' he said.

The four dead brothers clustered with Septimus at the window.

'What do you think he's thinking?' asked Quintus of Sextus.

'He's wondering where the stone fell, and how to reach it first,' said Sextus, remembering his fall down the rocks and into eternity.

'I damned well hope so,' said the late eighty-first master of Stormhold to his four dead sons. But his three sons who were not yet dead heard nothing at all.

* * *

A question like 'How big is Faerie?' does not admit of a simple answer.

Faerie, after all, is not one land, one principality or dominion. Maps of Faerie are unreliable, and may not be depended upon.

We talk of the Kings and Queens of Faerie as we would speak of the Kings and Queens of England. But Faerie is bigger than England, as it is bigger than the world (for, since the dawn of time, each land that has been forced off the map by explorers and the brave going out and proving it wasn't there has taken refuge in Faerie; so it is now, by the time that we come to write of it, a most huge place indeed, containing every manner of landscape and terrain). *Here*, truly, *there be Dragons*. Also gryphons, wyverns, hippogriffs, basilisks, and hydras. There are all manner of more familiar animals as well, cats affectionate and aloof, dogs noble and cowardly, wolves and foxes, eagles and bears.

In the middle of a wood so thick and so deep it was very nearly a forest was a small house, built of thatch and wood and daubed grey clay, which had a most foreboding aspect. A small, yellow bird in a cage sat on its perch outside the house. It did not sing, but sat mournfully silent, its feathers ruffled and wan. There was a door to the cottage, from which the once-white paint was peeling away.

Inside, the cottage consisted of one room, undivided. Smoked meats and sausages hung from the rafters, along with a wizened crocodile carcass. A peat fire burned smokily in the large fireplace against one wall, and the smoke trickled out of the chimney far above. There were three blankets upon three raised beds – one large and old, the other two little more than truckle beds.

There were cooking implements, and a large wooden cage, currently empty, in another corner. There were windows too filthy to see through, and over everything was a thick layer of oily dust.

The only thing in the house that was clean was a mirror of black glass, as high as a tall man, as wide as a church door, which rested against one wall.

The house belonged to three aged women. They took it in turns to sleep in the big bed, to make the supper, to set snares in the wood for small animals, to draw water up from the deep well behind the house.

The three women spoke little.

There were three other women in the little house. They were slim, and dark, and amused. The hall they inhabited was many times the size of the cottage; the floor was of onyx, and the pillars were of obsidian. There was a courtyard behind them, open to the sky, and stars hung in the night sky above. A fountain played in the courtyard, the water rolling and falling from a statue of a mermaid in ecstasy, her mouth wide open. Clean, black water gushed from her mouth into the pool below, shimmering and shaking the stars.

The three women, and their hall, were in the black mirror.

The three old women were the Lilim – the witch-queen – all alone in the woods.

The three women in the mirror were also the Lilim: but whether they were the successors to the old women, or their shadow-selves, or whether only the peasant cottage in the woods was real, or if, somewhere, the Lilim lived in a black hall, with a fountain in the shape of a mermaid playing in the courtyard of stars, none knew for certain, and none but the Lilim could say.

On this day, one crone came in from the woods, carrying a stoat, its throat a splash of red.

She placed it on the dusty chopping board and took a sharp knife. She cut it around at the arms and legs and neck, then, with one filthy hand, she pulled the skin off the creature, as if pulling a child from its pyjamas, and she dropped the naked thing onto the wooden chopping block.

'Entrails?' she asked, in a quavering voice.

The smallest, oldest, most tangle-headed of the women, rocking back and forth in a rocking chair, said, 'Might as well.'

The first old woman picked up the stoat by the head, and sliced it from neck to groin. Its innards tumbled out onto the cutting board, red and purple and plum-coloured, intestines and vital organs like wet jewels on the dusty wood.

The woman screeched, 'Come quick! Come quick!' Then she pushed gently at the stoat-guts with her knife, and screeched once more.

The crone in the rocking chair pulled herself to her feet. (In the mirror, a dark woman stretched and rose from her divan.) The last old woman, returning from the outhouse, scurried as fast as she could from the woods.

'What?' she said. 'What is it?'

(In the mirror, a third young woman rejoined the other two. Her breasts were small and high, and her eyes were dark.)

'Look,' gestured the first old woman, pointing with her knife.

Their eyes were the colourless grey of extreme age, and they squinted at the organs on the slab.

'At last,' said one of them, and 'About time,' said another.

'Which of us, then, to find it?' asked the third.

The three women closed their eyes, and three old hands stabbed into the stoat-guts on the board.

An old hand opened. 'I've a kidney.'

'I've his liver.'

The third hand opened. It belonged to the oldest of the Lilim. 'I've his heart,' she said, triumphantly.

'How will you travel?'

'In our old chariot, drawn by what I find at the cross-roads.'

'You'll be needing some years.'

The oldest one nodded.

The youngest, the one who had come in from the outhouse, walked, painfully slowly, over to a high and ramshackle chest of drawers, and bent over. She took a rusting iron box from the bottommost drawer, and carried it over to her sisters. It was tied around with three pieces of old string, each with a different knot in it. Each of the women unknotted her own piece of string, then the one who had carried the box opened the lid.

Something glittered golden in the bottom of the box.

'Not much left,' sighed the youngest of the Lilim, who had been old when the wood they lived in was still beneath the sea.

'Then it's a good thing that we've found a new one, isn't it?' said the oldest, tartly, and with that she thrust a clawed hand into the box. Something golden tried to avoid her hand, but she caught it, wiggling and glimmering, opened her mouth, and popped it inside.

(In the mirror, three women stared out.)

There was a shivering and a shuddering at the centre of all things.

(Now, two women stared from the black mirror.)

In the cottage, two old women stared, envy and hope mixing in their faces, at a tall, handsome woman with black hair and dark eyes and red, red lips.

'My,' she said, 'but this place is filthy.' She strode to the bed. Beside it was a large wooden chest, covered by a faded tapestry. She twitched off the tapestry, and opened the chest, rummaging inside.

'Here we go,' she said, holding up a scarlet kirtle. She tossed it onto the bed, and pulled off the rags and tatters she had worn as an old woman.

Her two sisters stared across at her naked body hungrily.

'When I return with her heart, there will be years aplenty for all of us,' she said, eyeing her sisters' hairy chins and hollow eyes with disfavour. She slipped a scarlet bracelet onto her wrist, in the shape of a small snake with its tail between its jaws.

'A star,' said one of her sisters.

'A star,' echoed the second.

'Exactly,' said the witch-queen, putting a circlet of silver upon her head. 'The first in two hundred years. And I'll bring it back to us.' She licked her scarlet lips with a deep red tongue.

'A fallen star,' she said.

***

It was night in the glade by the pool and the sky was bespattered with stars beyond counting.

Fireflies glittered in the leaves of the elm trees and in the ferns and in the hazel bushes, flickering on and off like the lights of a strange and distant city. An otter splashed in the brook that fed the pool. A family of stoats wove and wound their way to the water to drink. A fieldmouse found a fallen hazelnut and began to bite into the hard shell of the nut with its sharp, ever-growing front teeth, not because it was hungry, but because it was a prince under an enchantment who could not regain his outer form until he chewed the Nut of Wisdom. But its excitement made it careless, and only the shadow that blotted out the moonlight warned it of the descent of a huge grey owl, who caught the mouse in its sharp talons and rose again into the night.

The mouse dropped the nut, which fell into the brook and was carried away, to be swallowed by a salmon. The owl swallowed the mouse in just a couple of gulps, leaving just its tail trailing from her mouth, like a length of bootlace. Something snuffled and grunted as it pushed through the thicket – *a badger*, thought the owl (herself under a curse, and only able to resume her rightful shape if she consumed a mouse who had eaten the Nut of Wisdom), *or perhaps a small bear.*

Leaves rustled, water rilled, and then the glade became filled with light shining down from above, a pure white light which grew brighter and brighter. The owl saw it reflected in the pool, a blazing, glaring thing of pure light, so bright that she took to the wing and flew to another part of the forest. The wild things looked about them in terror.

First the light in the sky was no bigger than the moon, then it seemed larger, infinitely larger, and the whole grove trembled and quivered and every creature held its breath and the fireflies glowed brighter than they had ever glowed in their lives, each one convinced that *this* at last was love, but to no avail . . .

And then—

There was a cracking sound, sharp as a shot, and the light that had filled the grove was gone.

Or almost gone. There was a dim glow pulsing from the middle of the hazel thicket, as if a tiny cloud of stars were glimmering there.

And there was a voice, a high clear, female voice, which said, 'Ow,' and then, very quietly, it said 'Fuck,' and then it said 'Ow,' once more.

And then it said nothing at all, and there was silence in the glade.

Chapter Four

'Can I Get There by Candlelight?'

October moved further away with every step Tristran took; he felt as if he were walking into summer. There was a path through the woods, with a high hedgerow to one side, and he followed the path. High above him the stars glittered and gleamed, and the harvest moon shone golden yellow, the colour of ripe corn. In the moonlight he could see briar-roses in the hedge.

He was becoming sleepy now. For a time he fought to stay awake, and then he took off his overcoat, and put down his bag – a large leather bag of the kind that, in twenty years' time, would become known as a Gladstone bag – and he laid his head on his bag, and covered himself with his coat.

He stared up at the stars: and it seemed to him then that they were dancers, stately and graceful, performing a dance almost infinite in its complexity. He imagined he could see the very faces of the stars; pale, they were, and smiling gently, as if they had spent so much time above the world, watching the scrambling and the joy and the pain of the people below them, that they could not help being amused every time another little human believed itself the centre of its world, as each of us does.

And then it came to Tristran that he was dreaming, and he walked into his bedroom, which was also the schoolroom of the village of Wall: and Mrs Cherry tapped the blackboard and bade them all be silent, and Tristran looked down at his slate to see what the lesson would be about, but he could not read what he had written there. Then Mrs Cherry, who resembled his mother so much that Tristran found himself astonished he had never before realized that they were the same person, called upon Tristran to tell the class the dates of all the Kings and Queens of England . . .

' 'Scuse me,' said a small and hairy voice in his ear, 'but would you mind dreamin' a bit quieter? Your dreams is spillin' over into my dreams, and if there's one thing I've never been doin' with, it's dates. William the Conker, ten sixty-six, that's as far as I go, and I'd swap that for a dancing mouse.'

'Mm?' said Tristran.

'Keep it down,' said the voice. 'If you don't mind.'

'Sorry,' said Tristran, and his dreams after that were of the dark.

***

'Breakfast,' said a voice close to his ear. 'It's mushrumps, fried in butter, with wild garlic.'

Tristran opened his eyes: daylight shone through the briar-rose hedge, dappling the grass in gold and green. Something smelled like heaven.

A tin container was placed beside him.

'Poor fare,' said the voice. 'Country fare, it is. Nothing like the gentry are used to, but the likes of me treasures a fine mushrump.'

Tristran blinked, and reached into the tin bowl and took out a large mushroom between finger and thumb. It was hot.

He took a careful bite, felt the juices flood his mouth. It was the finest thing he had ever eaten and, after he had chewed and swallowed it, he said so.

'That's kind of you,' said the small figure who sat on the other side of a little fire which crackled and smoked in the morning air. 'Kind of you, I'm sure. But *you* know, and *I* know, that it's just fried field-mushrumps, and never a patch on nothing proper . . .'

'Is there any more?' asked Tristran, realizing just how hungry he was: sometimes a little food can do that to you.

'Ah now, that's manners for you,' said the little figure, who wore a large, floppy hat and a large, flappy overcoat. '*Is there more?* he says, as if it were poached quail's eggs and smoked gazelle and truffles, not just a mushrump what tastes more or less like something what's been dead for a week and a cat wouldn't touch. *Manners.*'

'I really, truly would like another mushroom,' said Tristran, 'if it's not too much trouble.'

The little man – if man he was, which Tristran found rather unlikely – sighed mournfully, and reached into the pan sizzling on the fire, with his knife, and flicked two large mushrooms into Tristran's tin bowl.

Tristran blew on them, then ate them with his fingers.

'Look at you,' said the little hairy person, his voice a mixture of pride and gloom, 'eatin' those mushrumps as if you liked them, as if they wasn't sawdust and wormwood and rue in your mouth.'

Tristran licked his fingers, and assured his benefactor that they had been the very finest mushrooms he had ever had the privilege of eating.

'You says that now,' said his host with gloomy relish, 'but you'll not be sayin' that in an hour's time. They'll undoubtedly disagree with you, like the fishwife who disagreed with her young man over a mermaid. And that could be heard from Garamond to Stormhold. Such language! It fair turned my ears blue, it did.' The little hairy

personage sighed deeply. 'Talkin' about your guts,' he said,
'I'm going to attend to mine behind that tree over there.
Would you do me the signal honour of keepin' an eye on that
there pack of mine? I'd be obliged.'

'Of course,' said Tristran, politely.

The little hairy man vanished behind an oak tree; Tristran
heard a few grunts, and then his new friend reappeared,
saying, 'There. I knowed a man in Paphlagonia who'd
swallow a live snake every morning, when he got up. He
used to say, he was certain of one thing, that nothing worse
would happen to him all day. 'Course they made him eat a
bowlful of hairy centipedes before they hung him, so maybe
that claim was a bit presumptive.'

Tristran excused himself. He urinated against the side of
the oak tree, next to which was a small mound of droppings,
certainly not produced by any human being. They looked
like deer pellets, or rabbit-droppings.

'My name is Tristran Thorn,' said Tristran, when he
returned. His breakfast companion had packed up the
morning's breakfast – fire, pans and all – and made it vanish
into his pack.

He removed his hat, pressed it to his chest, and looked up
at Tristran. 'Charmed,' he said. He tapped the side of his
pack: on it was written: CHARMED, ENCHANTED, ENSORCELLED
AND CONFUSTICATED. 'I used to be confusticated,' he confided,
'but you know how these things go.'

And with that he set off along the path. Tristran walked
behind him. 'Hey! I say!' called Tristran. 'Slow down, can't
you?' For despite the huge pack (which put Tristran in mind of
Christian's burden in *Pilgrim's Progress*, a book from which Mrs
Cherry had read to them every Monday morning, telling them
that, although it was written by a tinker, it was a fine book for
all of that) the little man – Charmed? Was that his name? – was
moving away from him as fast as a squirrel up a tree.

The little creature hurried back down the path. 'Somethin'
wrong?' he asked.

'I cannot keep up,' confessed Tristran. 'You walk so con-
foundedly fast.'

The little hairy man slowed his pace. 'Beg your puddin','
he said, as Tristran stumbled after him. 'Bein' on me own so
much, I gets used to settin' me own pace.'

They walked side by side, in the golden-green light of the
sun through the newly opened leaves. It was a quality of
light Tristran had observed, unique to springtime. He
wondered if they had left summer as far behind as October.
From time to time Tristran would remark on a flash of colour
in a tree or bush, and the little hairy man would say
something like, 'Kingfisher. Mr Halcyon they used to call
him. Pretty bird,' or 'Purple hummingbird. Drinks nectar
from flowers. Hovers,' or 'Redcap. They'll keep their
distance, but don't you go scrutinizin' 'em or looking for
trouble, 'cos you'll find it with those buggers.'

They sat beside a brook to eat their lunch. Tristran
produced the cottage loaf, the ripe, red apples, and round of
cheese – hard, tart and crumbly – that his mother had given
him. And although the little man eyed them all suspiciously,
he wolfed them down and licked the crumbs of bread and
cheese from his fingers, and munched noisily on the apple.
Then he filled a kettle from the brook, and boiled it up for tea.

'Suppose you tell me what you're about?' said the little
hairy man as they sat on the ground and drank their tea.

Tristran thought for some moments, and then he said, 'I
come from the village of Wall, where there lives a young lady
named Victoria Forester, who is without peer among women,
and it is to her, and to her alone, that I have given my heart.
Her face is—'

'Usual complement of bits?' asked the little creature.
'Eyes? Nose? Teeth? All the usual?'

'Of course.'

'Well then, you can skip that stuff,' said the little hairy
man. 'We'll take it all as said. So what damn-fool silly thing
has this young lady got you a-doin' of?'

Tristran put down his wooden cup of tea, and stood up, offended.

'What,' he asked, in what he was certain were lofty and scornful tones, 'would possibly make you imagine that my lady-love would have sent me on some foolish errand?'

The little man stared up at him with eyes like beads of jet. 'Because that's the only reason a lad like you would be stupid enough to cross the border into Faerie. The only ones who ever come here from your lands are the minstrels, and the lovers, and the mad. And you don't look like much of a minstrel, and you're – pardon me saying so, lad, but it's true – ordinary as cheese-crumbs. So it's love, if you ask me.'

'Because,' announced Tristran, 'every lover is in his heart a madman, and in his head a minstrel.'

'Really?' said the little man, doubtfully. 'I'd never noticed. So there's some young lady. Has she sent you here to seek your fortune? That used to be very popular. You'd get young fellers wanderin' all over, looking for the hoard of gold that some poor wyrm or ogre had taken absolute centuries to accumulate.'

'No. Not my fortune. It was more of a promise I made to this lady I mentioned. I . . . we were talking, and I was promising her things, and we saw this falling star, and I promised to bring it to her. And it fell . . .' he waved an arm toward a mountain range somewhere in the general direction of the sunrise '. . . over there.'

The little hairy man scratched his chin. Or his muzzle; it might well have been his muzzle. 'You know what I would do?'

'No,' said Tristran, hope rising within him, 'what?'

The little man wiped his nose. 'I'd tell her to go shove her face in the pig pen, and go out and find another one who'll kiss you without askin' for the earth. You're bound to find one. You can hardly throw half a brick back in the lands you come from without hittin' one.'

'There *are* no other girls,' said Tristran definitely.

The little man sniffed, and they packed up their things and walked on together.

'Did you mean it?' said the little man. 'About the fallen star?'

'Yes,' said Tristran.

'Well, I'd not mention it about if I were you,' said the little man. 'There's those as would be unhealthily interested in such information. Better keep mum. But never lie.'

'So what should I say?'

'Well,' he said, 'f'r example, if they ask where you've come from, you could say "Behind me," and if they asked where you're going, you'd say "In front of me." '

'I see,' said Tristran, unimpressed.

The path they were walking became harder to discern. A cold breeze ruffled Tristran's hair, and he shivered. The path led them into a grey wood of thin, pale birch trees.

'Do you think it will be far?' asked Tristran. 'To the star?'

'How many miles to Babylon?' said the little man rhetorically. 'This wood wasn't here, last time I was by this way,' he added.

'*How Many Miles to Babylon*,' recited Tristran, to himself, as they walked through the grey wood.

'*Three score miles and ten.*
Can I get there by candlelight?
There, and back again.
Yes, if your feet are nimble and light,
You can get there by candlelight.'

'That's the one,' said the little hairy man, his head questing from side to side as if he were preoccupied, or a little nervous.

'It's only a nursery rhyme,' said Tristran.

'Only a *nursery* . . .? Bless me, there's some on this side of the wall would give seven years' hard toil for that little cantrip. And back where you come from you mutter 'em to babes alongside of a "Rock-a-Bye-Baby" or a "Rub-a-Dub-Dub," without a second thought . . . Are you chilled, lad?'

'Now that you mention it, I am a bit cold, yes.'

'Look around you. Can you see a path?'

Tristran blinked. The grey wood soaked up light and colour and distance. He had thought they were following a path, but now that he tried to see the path, it shimmered, and vanished, like an optical illusion. He had taken *that* tree, and *that* tree, and *that* rock as markers of the path . . . but there was no path, only the mirk, and the twilight, and the pale trees. 'Now we're for it,' said the hairy man, in a small voice.

'Should we run?' Tristran removed his bowler hat, and held it in front of him.

The little man shook his head. 'Not much point,' he said. 'We've walked into the trap, and we'll still be in it even if we runs.'

He walked over to the nearest tree, a tall, pale, birchlike tree trunk, and kicked it, hard. Some dry leaves fell, and then something white tumbled from the branches to the earth with a dry, whispering sound.

Tristran walked over to it and looked down; it was the skeleton of a bird, clean and white and dry.

The little man shivered. 'I could castle,' he told Tristran, 'but there's no one I could castle with'd be any better off here than we are . . . There's no escape by flying, not judgin' by *that* thing.' He nudged the skeleton with one pawlike foot. 'And your sort of people never could learn to burrow – not that that'd do us much good . . .'

'Perhaps we could arm ourselves,' said Tristran.

'Arm ourselves?'

'Before they come.'

'Before they *come*? Why – they're *here*, you puddenhead. It's the trees themselves. We're in a serewood.'

'Serewood?'

'It's me own fault – I should've been paying more attention to where we was goin'. Now you'll never get your star, and

I'll never get my merchandise. One day some other poor bugger lost in the wood'll find our skellingtons picked clean as whistles and that'll be that.'

Tristran stared about him. In the gloom it seemed that the trees were crowding about more thickly, although he had seen nothing actually move. He wondered if the little man were being foolish, or imagining things.

Something stung his left hand. He slapped at it, expecting to see an insect. He looked down to see a pale yellow leaf. It fell to the ground with a rustle. On the back of his hand, a veining of red, wet blood welled up. The wood whispered about them.

'Is there anything we can do?' Tristran asked.

'Nothing I can think of. If only we knew where the true path was . . . even a serewood couldn't destroy the true path. Just hide it from us, lure us off of it . . .' The little man shrugged, and sighed.

Tristran reached his hand up and rubbed his forehead. 'I . . . I *do* know where the path is,' he said. He pointed. 'It's down that way.'

The little man's bead-black eyes glittered. 'Are you sure?'

'Yes, sir. Through that copse and up a little way to the right. That's where the path is.'

'How do you know?' asked the man.

'I *know*,' replied Tristran.

'Right. Come on!' And the little man took his burden and ran, slowly enough that Tristran, his leather bag swinging and banging against his legs, his heart pounding, his breath coming in gasps, was able to keep up.

'No! Not that way. Over to the left!' shouted Tristran. Branches and thorns ripped and tore at his clothes. They ran on in silence.

The trees seemed to have arranged themselves into a wall. Leaves fell around them in flurries, stinging and smarting when they touched Tristran's skin, cutting and slicing at his clothes. He clambered up the hill, swiping at the leaves with his free hand, swatting at the twigs and branches with his bag.

The silence was broken by something wailing. It was the little hairy man. He had stopped dead where he stood, and, his head thrown back, had begun to howl at the sky.

'Buck up,' said Tristran. 'We're nearly there.' He grasped the little hairy man's free hand in his own larger hand, and pulled him forward.

And then they were standing on the true path: a swath of green sward running through the grey wood. 'Are we safe here?' asked Tristran, panting, and looking about apprehensively.

'We're safe, as long as we stay on the path,' said the little hairy man, and he put down his burden, sat down on the grass of the path and stared at the trees about them.

The pale trees shook, although no wind blew, and it seemed to Tristran that they shook in anger.

His companion had begun to shudder, his hairy fingers raking and stroking the green grass. Then he looked up at Tristran. 'I don't suppose you have such a thing as a bottle of something spirituous upon you? Or perchance a pot of hot, sweet tea?'

'No,' said Tristran. ' 'fraid not.'

The little man sniffed, and fumbled at the lock of his huge package. 'Turn round,' he said to Tristran. 'No peekin'.'

Tristran turned away.

There was a rummaging, scuffling noise. Then the sound of a lock clicking shut, and then, 'You can turn around, if you like.' The little man was holding an enamel bottle. He was tugging, vainly, at the stopper.

'Um.~Would you like me to help you with that?' Tristran hoped the little hairy man would not be offended by his request. He should not have worried; his companion thrust the bottle into his hands.

'Here go,' he said. 'You've got the fingers for it.'

Tristran tugged and pulled out the stopper of the bottle. He could smell something intoxicating, like honey mixed with wood smoke and cloves. He passed the bottle back to the little man.

'It's a crime to drink something as rare and good as this out of the bottle,' said the little hairy man. He untied the little wooden cup from his belt, and, trembling, poured a small amount of an amber-coloured liquid into it. He sniffed it, then sipped it, then he smiled, with small, sharp teeth.

'Aaaahhhh. That's better.'

He passed the cup to Tristran.

'Sip it slowly,' he said. 'It's worth a king's ransom, this bottle. It cost me two large blue-white diamonds, a mechanical bluebird which sang, and a dragon's scale.'

Tristran sipped the drink. It warmed him down to his toes and made him feel like his head was filled with tiny bubbles.

'Good, eh?'

Tristran nodded.

'Too good for the likes of you and me, I'm afraid. Still. It hits the spot in times of trouble, of which this is certainly one. Let's get out of this wood,' said the little hairy man. 'Which way, though . . .?'

'That way,' said Tristran, pointing to their left.

The little man stoppered and pocketed the little bottle, shouldered his pack, and the two of them walked together down the green path through the grey wood.

After several hours, the white trees began to thin, and then they were through the serewood and walking between two low rough-stone walls, along a high bank. When Tristran looked back the way they had come there was no sign of any wood at all; the way behind them was purple-headed, heathery hills.

'We can stop here,' said his companion. 'There's stuff we needs to talk about. Sit down.'

He put down his enormous bag, and climbed on top of it, so he was looking down at Tristran, who sat on a rock beside the road. 'There's something here I'm not properly gettin'. Now, tell me. Where are you from?'

'Wall,' said Tristran. 'I *told* you.'

'Who's your father and mother?'

'My father's name is Dunstan Thorn. My mother is Daisy Thorn.'

'Mmm. Dunstan Thorn . . . Mm. I met your father once. He put me up for the night. Not a bad chap, although he doesn't half go on a bit while a fellow's trying to get a little kip.' He scratched his muzzle. 'Still doesn't explain . . . there isn't anythin' *unusual* in your family, is there?'

'My sister, Louisa, can wiggle her ears.'

The little hairy man wiggled his own large, hairy ears, dismissively. 'No, that's not it,' he said. 'I was thinkin' more of a grandmother who was a famous enchantress, or an uncle who was a prominent warlock, or a brace of fairies somewhere in the family tree.'

'None that I know of,' admitted Tristran.

The little man changed his tack. 'Where's the village of Wall?' he asked. Tristran pointed. 'Where are the Debatable Hills?' Tristran pointed once more, without hesitation. 'Where's the Catavarian Isles?' Tristran pointed to the south-west. He had not known there *were* Debatable Hills, or Catavarian Isles until the little man had mentioned them, but he was as certain in himself of their location as he was of the whereabouts of his own left foot or the nose on his face.

'Hmm. Now then. Do you know where His Vastness the Freemartin Muskish is?'

Tristran shook his head.

'D'you know where His Vastness the Freemartin Muskish's Transluminary Citadel is?'

Tristran pointed, with certainty.

'And what of Paris? The one in France?'

Tristran thought for a moment. 'Well, if Wall's over there, I suppose that Paris must be sort of in the same sort of direction, mustn't it.'

'Let's see,' said the little hairy man, talking to himself as much as to Tristran. 'You can find places in Faerie, but not in your world, save for Wall, and that's a boundary. You can't find people . . . but . . . tell me, lad, can you find this star you're lookin' for?'

Tristran pointed, immediately. 'It's that way,' he said.

'Hmm. That's good. But it still doesn't explain nuffink. You hungry?'

'A bit. And I'm tattered and torn,' said Tristran, fingering the huge holes in his trousers, and in his coat, where the branches and the thorns had seized at him, and the leaves had cut at him as he ran. 'And look at my boots . . .'

'What's in your bag?'

Tristran opened his Gladstone bag. 'Apples. Cheese. Half a cottage loaf. And a pot of fishpaste. My penknife. I've got a change of underwear, and a couple of pairs of woolen socks. I suppose I should have brought more clothes . . .'

'Keep the fishpaste,' said his travelling companion, and he rapidly divided the remaining food into two equal piles.

'You done me a good turn,' he said, munching a crisp apple, 'and I doesn't forget something like that. First we'll get your clothes took care of, and then we'll send you off after your star. Yus?'

'That's extremely kind of you,' said Tristran, nervously, slicing his cheese onto his crust of bread.

'Right,' said the little hairy man. 'Let's find you a blanket.'

* * *

At dawn three lords of Stormhold rode down the craggy mountain road, in a coach pulled by six black horses. The horses wore bobbing black plumes, the coach was fresh painted in black, and each of the lords of Stormhold was dressed in mourning.

In the case of Primus, this took the shape of a long, black, monkish robe; Tertius was dressed in the sober costume of a

merchant in mourning; while Septimus wore a black doublet
and hose, a black hat with a black feather in it, and looked
for all the world like a foppish assassin from a minor
Elizabethan historical play.

The lords of Stormhold eyed each other, one cautious, one
wary, one blank. They said nothing: had alliances been
possible, Tertius might have sided with Primus against
Septimus. But there were no alliances that could be made.

The carriage clattered and shook.

Once, it stopped, for each of the three lords to relieve
himself. Then it clattered on down the hilly road. Together,
the three lords of Stormhold had placed their father's
remains in the Hall of Ancestors. Their dead brothers had
watched them from the doors of the hall, but had said
nothing.

Toward evening, the coachman called out, 'Nottaway!' and
he reined his team outside a tumbledown inn, built against
what resembled the ruins of a giant's cottage.

The three lords of Stormhold got out of the coach, and
stretched their cramped legs. Faces peered at them through
the bottle-glass windows of the inn.

The innkeeper, who was a choleric gnome of poor
disposition, looked out of the door. 'We'll need beds aired,
and a pot of mutton stew on the fire,' he called.

'How many beds to be aired?' asked Letitia the
chambermaid, from the stairwell.

'Three,' said the gnome. 'For I'll wager they'll have their
coachman sleep with the horses.'

'Three indeed,' whispered Tilly, the pot-girl, to Lacey, the
ostler, 'when anyone could see a full seven of those fine
gentlemen standing in the road.'

But when the lords of Stormhold entered there were but
three of them, and they announced that their coachman
would sleep in the stables.

Dinner was mutton stew, and bread loaves so hot and fresh
they exhaled steam as they were cracked open, and each of

the lords took an unopened bottle of the finest Baragundian wine (for none of the lords would share a bottle with his fellows, nor even permit the wine to be poured from the bottle into a goblet). This scandalized the gnome, who was of the opinion – *not*, however, uttered in the hearing of his guests – that the wine should be permitted to breathe.

Their coachman ate his bowl of stew, and drank two pots of ale, and went to sleep in the stables. The three brothers went to their respective rooms and barred the doors.

Tertius had slipped a silver coin to Letitia the chambermaid when she had brought him the warming-pan for his bed, so he was not surprised at all when, shortly before midnight, there came a tap-tapping on his door.

She wore a one-piece white chemise, and curtsied to him as he opened the door, and smiled, shyly. She held a bottle of wine in her hand.

He locked the door behind him, and led her to the bed, where, having first made her remove her chemise, and having examined her face and body by candlelight, and having kissed her on the forehead, lips, nipples, navel and toes, and having extinguished the candle, he made love to her, without speaking, in the pale moonlight.

After some time, he grunted, and was still.

'There, lovey, was that good, now?' asked Letitia.

'Yes,' said Tertius, warily, as if her words guarded some trap. 'It was.'

'Would you be wanting another turn, before I leave?'

In reply, Tertius pointed between his legs. Letitia giggled. 'We can have *him* upstanding again in a twinkling,' she said. And she pulled out the cork from the bottle of wine she had carried in, and had placed beside the bed, and passed it to Tertius.

He grinned at her, and gulped down some wine, then pulled her to him.

'I bet that feels good,' she said to him. 'Now, lovey, *this* time let me show you how *I* like it . . . why, whatever is the matter?' For Lord Tertius of Stormhold was writhing back and forth on the bed, his eyes wide, his breathing laboured.

'That wine?' he gasped. 'Where did you get it?'

'Your brother,' said Letty. 'I met him on the stairs. He told me it was a fine restorative and stiffener, and it would provide us with a night we should never forget.'

'And so it has,' breathed Tertius, and he twitched, once, twice, three times, and then was stiff. And very still.

Tertius heard Letitia begin to scream, as if from a very long way away. He was conscious of four familiar presences, standing with him in the shadows beside the wall.

'She was very beautiful,' whispered Secundus, and Letitia thought she heard the curtains rustle.

'Septimus is most crafty,' said Quintus. 'That was the self-same preparation of baneberries he slipped into my dish of eels,' and Letitia thought she heard the wind, howling down from the mountain crags.

She opened the door to the household, woken by her screams, and a search ensued. Lord Septimus, however, was nowhere to be found, and one of the black stallions was gone from the stable (in which the coachman slept and snored and could not be wakened).

Lord Primus was in a foul mood when he arose the next morning.

He declined to have Letitia put to death, stating she was as much a victim of Septimus's craft as Tertius had been, but ordered that she accompany Tertius's body back to the castle of Stormhold.

He left her one black horse to carry the body, and a pouch of silver coins. It was enough to pay a villager of Nottaway to travel with her – to ensure no wolves made off with the horse or his brother's remains – and to pay off the coachman when finally he awoke.

And then, alone in the coach, pulled by a team of four coal-black stallions, Lord Primus left the village of Nottaway, in significantly worse temper than he had arrived there.

***

Brevis arrived at the crossroads tugging at a rope. The rope was attached to a bearded, horned, evil-eyed billy goat, which Brevis was taking to market to sell.

That morning, Brevis's mother had placed a single radish upon the table in front of him and had said, 'Brevis, son. This radish was all I was able to pull from the ground today. All our crops have failed, and all our food has gone. We've nothing to sell but the billy goat. So I want you to halter the goat, and take him to the market, and sell him to a farmer. And with the coins you get for the goat – and you'll take nothing less than a florin, mark you – buy a hen, and buy corn, and turnips; and perhaps we shall not starve.'

So Brevis had chewed his radish, which was woody, and peppery to the tongue, and spent the rest of the morning chasing the goat about its pen, sustaining a bruise to the rib and a bite to the thigh in the process, and, eventually, and with the help of a passing tinker, he had subdued the goat enough to have it haltered, and leaving his mother to bandage the tinker's goat-inflicted injuries, he dragged the billy goat toward the market.

Sometimes the goat would take it into his head to charge on ahead, and Brevis would be dragged behind him, the heels of his boots grinding into the dried mud of the roadway, until the goat would decide – suddenly and without warning, for no reason Brevis was able to discern – to stop. Then Brevis would pick himself up and return to dragging the beast.

He reached the crossroads on the edge of the wood, sweaty and hungry and bruised, pulling an uncooperative goat. There was a tall woman standing at the crossroads. A circlet of silver sat in the crimson headpiece that surrounded her dark hair, and her dress was as scarlet as her lips.

'What do they call you, boy?' she asked, in a voice like musky brown honey.

'They call me Brevis, ma'am,' said Brevis, observing something strange behind the woman. It was a small cart, but there was nothing harnessed between the shafts. He wondered how it had ever got there.

'Brevis,' she purred. 'Such a nice name. Would you like to sell me your goat, Brevis-boy?'

Brevis hesitated. 'My mother told me I was to take the goat to the market,' he said, 'and to sell him for a hen, and some corn, and some turnips, and to bring her home the change.'

'How much did your mother tell you to take for the goat?' asked the woman in the scarlet kirtle.

'Nothing less than a florin,' he said.

She smiled, and held up one hand. Something glinted yellow. 'Why, I will give you this golden guinea,' she said, 'enough to buy a coopful of hens and a hundred bushels of turnips.'

The boy's mouth hung open.

'Do we have a deal?'

The boy nodded, and thrust out the hand which held the billy goat's rope halter. 'Here,' was all he could say, visions of limitless wealth and turnips beyond counting tumbling through his head.

The lady took the rope. Then she touched one finger to the goat's forehead, between its yellow eyes, and let go of the rope.

Brevis expected the billy goat to bolt for the woods or down one of the roads, but it stayed where it was, as if frozen into position. Brevis held out his hand for the golden guinea.

The woman looked at him then, examining him from the soles of his muddy feet to his sweaty, cropped hair, and once more she smiled.

'You know,' she said, 'I think that a matched pair would be so much more impressive than just one. Don't you?'

Brevis did not know what she was talking about, and opened his mouth to tell her so. But just then she reached out one long finger, and touched the bridge of his nose, between his eyes, and he found he could not say anything at all.

She snapped her fingers, and Brevis and the billy goat hastened to stand between the shafts of her cart; and Brevis was surprised to notice that he was walking on four legs, and he seemed to be no taller than the animal beside him.

The witch-woman cracked her whip, and her cart jolted off down the muddy road, drawn by a matched pair of horned white billy goats.

***

The little hairy man had taken Tristran's ripped coat and trousers and waistcoat, and, leaving him covered by a blanket, had walked into the village which nestled in the valley between three heather-covered hills.

Tristran sat under the blanket, in the warm evening, and waited.

Lights flickered in the hawthorn bush behind him. He thought they were glow-worms or fireflies, but, on closer inspection, he perceived they were tiny people, flickering and flitting from branch to branch.

He coughed, politely. A score of tiny eyes stared down at him. Several of the little creatures vanished. Others retreated high into the hawthorn bush, while a handful, braver than the others, flitted towards him.

They began to laugh, in high, bell-tinkling tones, pointing at Tristran, in his broken boots and blanket, and under-clothes, and bowler hat. Tristran blushed red, and pulled the blanket about himself.

One of the little folk sang:

Hankety pankety
Boy in a blanket, he's
Off on a goose-chase to
Look for a star

Incontrovertibly
Journeys through Fäerie
Strip off the blanket to
See who you are.

And another one sang:

Tristran Thorn
Tristran Thorn
Does not know why he was born
And a foolish oath has sworn
Trews and coat and shirt are torn
So he sits here all forlorn
Soon to face his true love's scorn
Wistran
Bistran
Tristran
Thorn.

'Be off with you, you silly things,' said Tristran, his face burning, and, having nothing else to hand, he threw his bowler hat at them.

Thus it was, that when the little hairy man arrived back from the village of Revelry (although why it was so called no man alive could say, for it was a gloomy, sombre place, and had been for time out of mind) he found Tristran sitting glumly beside a hawthorn bush, wrapped in a blanket, and bewailing the loss of his hat.

'They said cruel things about my true love,' said Tristran. 'Miss Victoria Forester. How dare they?'

'The little folk dare anything,' said his friend. 'And they talks a lot of nonsense. But they talks an awful lot of sense, as well. You listen to 'em at your peril, and you ignore 'em at your peril, too.'

'They said I was soon to face my true love's scorn.'

'Did they, indeed?' The little hairy man was laying a

variety of clothes out upon the grass. Even in the moonlight, Tristran could see that the clothes he was laying out bore no manner of resemblance to the clothes that Tristran had removed earlier in the day.

In the village of Wall, men wore brown, and grey, and black; and even the reddest neckerchief worn by the ruddiest of farmers was soon faded by the sun and the rain to a more mannerly colour. Tristran looked at the crimson and canary and russet cloth, at clothes which looked more like the costumes of travelling players or the contents of his cousin Joan's charades chest, and said, 'My clothes?'

'These are your clothes now,' said the little hairy man, proudly. 'I traded 'em. This stuff's better quality – see, it won't rip and tear as easy – and it's neither tattered nor torn, and withal, you'll not stick out so much as a stranger. This is what people wears hereabouts, y'see.'

Tristran contemplated making the rest of his quest wrapped in a blanket, like a savage aboriginal from one of his schoolbooks. Then, with a sigh, he took off his boots, and let the blanket fall to the grass, and, with the little hairy man as his guide ('No, no, laddie, those go *over* that. Mercy, what do they teach them nowadays?') he was soon dressed in his fine new clothes.

The new boots fit him better than the old ones ever had.

They certainly *were* fine new clothes. While clothes do not, as the saying would sometimes have it, make the man, and fine feathers do not make fine birds, sometimes they can add a certain spice to a recipe. And Tristran Thorn in crimson and canary was not the same man that Tristran Thorn in his overcoat and Sunday suit had been. There was a swagger to his steps, a jauntiness to his movements, that had not been there before. His chin went up instead of down, and there was a glint in his eye that he had not possessed when he had worn a bowler hat.

By the time they had eaten the meal the little hairy man had brought back with him from Revelry – which consisted of smoked trout, a bowl of fresh shelled peas, several small raisin-cakes, and a bottle of small beer – Tristran felt quite at home with his new garb.

'Now then,' said the little hairy man. 'You've saved my life, laddie, back there in the serewood, and your father, he done me a good turn back before you was born, and let it never be said that I'm a cove what doesn't pay his debts—' Tristran began to mutter something about how his friend had already done more than enough for him, but the little hairy man ignored him and continued, '—so I was a-ponderin': you know where your star is, don't you?'

Tristran pointed, without hesitation, to the dark horizon.

'Now then, *how far* is it, to your star? D'you know that?'

Tristran had not given the matter any thought, hitherto, but he found himself saying, 'A man could walk, only stopping to sleep, while the moon waxed and waned above him a half a dozen times, crossing treacherous mountains and burning deserts, before he reached the place where the star has fallen.'

It did not sound like the kind of thing that he would say at all, and he blinked with surprise.

'As I thought,' said the little hairy man, approaching his burden, and bending over it, so Tristran could not see how it unlocked. 'And it's not like you're the only one'll be lookin' for it. You remember what I told you before?'

'About digging a hole to bury my dung in?'

'Not that.'

'About telling no one my true name, nor my destination?'

'Nor yet that.'

'Then what?'

'*How many miles to Babylon?*' recited the man.

'Oh. Yes. That.'

'*Can I get there by candlelight? There and back again*. Only it's the candle-wax, you see. Most candles won't do it. This one took a lot of findin'.' And he pulled out a candle-stub the size of a crabapple, and handed it to Tristran.

Tristran could see nothing in any way out of the ordinary about the candle-stub. It was a wax candle, not tallow, and it was much used and melted. The wick was charred and black.

'What do I do with it?' he asked.

'All in good time,' said the little hairy man, and took something else from his pack. 'Take this, too. You'll need it.'

It glittered in the moonlight. Tristran took it; the little man's gift seemed to be a thin silver chain, with a loop at each end. It was cold and slippery to the touch. 'What is it?'

'The usual. Cat's breath and fish-scales and moonlight on a mill-pond, melted and smithied and forged by the dwarfs. You'll be needin' it to bring your star back with you.'

'I will?'

'Oh, yes.'

Tristran let the chain fall into his palm: it felt like quicksilver. 'Where do I keep it? I have no pockets in these confounded clothes.'

'Wrap it around your wrist until you need it. Like that. There you go. But you've a pocket in your tunic, under there, see?'

Tristran found the concealed pocket. Above it there was a small buttonhole, and in the buttonhole he placed the snowdrop, the glass flower that his father had given him as a luck token when he had left Wall. He wondered whether it was in fact bringing him luck, and if it were, was it good luck or bad?

Tristran stood up. He held his leather bag tightly in his hand.

'Now then,' said the little hairy man. 'This is what you got to do. Take up the candle in your right hand; I'll light it for you. And then, walk to your star. You'll use the chain to bring it back here. There's not much wick left on the candle, so you'd best be snappy about it, and step lively – any dawdlin' and you'll regret it. *Feet be nimble and light*, yes?'

'I . . . I suppose so, yes,' said Tristran.

He stood expectantly. The little hairy man passed a hand over the candle, which lit with a flame yellow above and blue below. There was a gust of wind, but the flame did not flicker even the slightest bit.

Tristran took the candle in his hand, and he began to walk forward. The candlelight illuminated the world: every tree and bush and blade of grass.

With Tristran's next step he was standing beside a lake, and the candlelight shone brightly on the water; and then he was walking through the mountains, through lonely crags, where the candlelight was reflected in the eyes of the creatures of the high snows; and then he was walking through the clouds, which, while not entirely substantial, still supported his weight in comfort; and then, holding tightly to his candle, he was underground, and the candlelight glinted back at him from the wet cave walls; now he was in the mountains once more; and then he was on a road through wild forest, and he glimpsed a chariot being pulled by two goats, being driven by a woman in a red dress who looked, for the glimpse he got of her, the way Boadicea was drawn in his history books; and another step and he was in a leafy glen, and he could hear the chuckle of water as it splashed and sang its way into a small brook.

He took another step, but he was still in the glen. There were high ferns, and elm trees, and foxgloves in abundance, and the moon had set in the sky. He held up the candle, looking for a fallen star, a rock, perhaps, or a jewel, but he saw nothing.

He heard something, though, under the babbling of the brook: a sniffling, and a swallowing. The sound of someone trying not to cry.

'Hello?' said Tristran.

The sniffling stopped. But Tristran was certain he could see a light beneath a hazel tree, and he walked toward it.

'Excuse me,' he said, hoping to pacify whoever was sitting beneath the hazel tree, and praying that it was not more of the little people who had stolen his hat. 'I'm looking for a star.'

In reply, a clod of wet earth flew out from under the tree, hitting Tristran on the side of the face. It stung a little, and fragments of earth fell down his collar and under his clothes.

'I won't hurt you,' he said, loudly.

This time, as another clod of earth came hurtling toward him, he ducked out of the way, and it smashed into an elm tree behind him. He walked forward.

'Go away,' said a voice, all raw and gulping, as if it had just been crying, 'just go away and leave me alone.'

She was sprawled, awkwardly, beneath the hazel tree, and she gazed up at Tristran with a scowl of complete unfriendliness. She hefted another clod of mud at him, menacingly, but did not throw it.

Her eyes were red and raw. Her hair was so fair it was almost white, her dress was of blue silk which shimmered in the candlelight. She glittered as she sat there. 'Please don't throw any more mud at me,' pleaded Tristran. 'Look. I didn't mean to disturb you. It's just there's a star fallen somewhere around here, and I have to get it back before the candle burns out.'

'I broke my leg,' said the young lady.

'I'm sorry, of course,' said Tristran. 'But the *star*.'

'I broke my leg,' she told him sadly, 'when I fell.' And with that, she heaved her lump of mud at him. Glittering dust fell from her arm, as it moved.

The clod of mud hit Tristran in the chest.

'Go away,' she sobbed, burying her face in her arms. 'Go away and leave me alone.'

'You're the star,' said Tristran, comprehension dawning.

'And you're a clodpoll,' said the girl, bitterly, 'and a ninny, a numbskull, a lackwit and a coxcomb!'

'Yes,' said Tristran. 'I suppose I am at that.' And with that he unwound one end of the silver chain, and slipped it around the girl's slim wrist. He felt the loop of the chain tighten about his own.

She stared up at him, bitterly. 'What,' she asked, in a voice that was suddenly beyond outrage, beyond hate, 'do you think you are doing?'

'Taking you home with me,' said Tristran. 'I made an oath.'

And at that the candle-stub guttered, violently, the last of the wick afloat in the pool of wax. For a moment the candle flame flared high, illuminating the glen, and the girl, and the chain, unbreakable, that ran from her wrist to his.

Then the candle went out.

Tristran stared at the star – at the girl – and, with all his might, managed to say nothing at all.

Can I get there by candlelight? he thought. *There, and back again.* But the candlelight was gone, and the village of Wall was six months' hard travel from here.

'I just want you to know,' said the girl, coldly, 'that whoever you are, and whatever you intend with me, I shall give you no aid of any kind, nor shall I assist you, and I shall do whatever is in my power to frustrate your plans and devices.' And then she added, with feeling, 'Idiot.'

'Mm,' said Tristran. 'Can you walk?'

'No,' she said. 'My leg's broken. Are you deaf, as well as stupid?'

'Do your kind sleep?' he asked her.

'Of course. But not at night. At night, we shine.'

'Well,' he said, 'I'm going to try to get some sleep. I can't think of anything else to do. It's been a long day for me, what with everything. And maybe you should try to sleep, too. We've got a long way to go.'

The sky was beginning to lighten. Tristran put his head on his leather bag in the glen, and did his best to ignore the insults and imprecations that came his way from the girl in the blue dress at the end of the chain.

He wondered what the little hairy man would do, when Tristran did not return.

He wondered what Victoria Forester was doing at the moment, and decided that she was probably asleep, in her bed, in her bedroom, in her father's farmhouse.

He wondered whether six months was a long walk, and what they would eat on the way.

He wondered what stars ate . . .

And then he was asleep.

'Dunderhead. Bumpkin. Dolt,' said the star.

And then she sighed, and made herself as comfortable as she could, under the circumstances. The pain from her leg was dull but continual. She tested the chain about her wrist, but it was tight and fast, and she could neither slip from it nor break it. 'Cretinous, verminous oaf,' she muttered.

And then she, too, slept.

Chapter Five

In Which There is Much Fighting for the Crown

In the morning's bright light the young lady seemed more human and less ethereal. She had said nothing since Tristran had woken.

He took his knife and cut a fallen tree branch into a Y-shaped crutch while she sat beneath a sycamore tree and glared at him and glowered at him and scowled at him from her place on the ground. He peeled the bark from a green branch and wound it around the upper fork of the Y.

They had had no breakfast yet, and Tristran was ravenous; his stomach rumbled as he worked. The star had said nothing about being hungry. Then again, she had done nothing at all but look at him, first reproachfully, and then with undisguised hatred.

He pulled the bark tight, then looped it under itself and tugged on it once more. 'This is honestly nothing personal,' he said, to the woman and to the grove. With the full sunlight shining down she scarcely glittered at all, save for where the darkest shadows touched her.

The star ran one pale forefinger up and down the silver

chain that went between them, tracing the line of it about her slim wrist, and made no reply.

'I did it for love,' he continued. 'And you really are my only hope. Her name – that is, the name of my love – is Victoria. Victoria Forester. And she is the prettiest, wisest, sweetest girl in the whole wide world.'

The girl broke her silence with a snort of derision. 'And this wise, sweet creature sent you here to torture me?' she said.

'Well, not exactly. You see, she promised me anything I desired – be it her hand in marriage or her lips to kiss – were I to bring her the star that we saw fall the night before last. I had thought,' he confessed, 'that a fallen star would probably look like a diamond or a rock. I certainly wasn't expecting a lady.'

'So, having found a lady, could you not have come to her aid, or left her alone? Why drag her into your foolishness?'

'Love,' he explained.

She looked at him with eyes the blue of the sky. 'I hope you choke on it,' she said, flatly.

'I won't,' said Tristran, with more confidence and good cheer than he actually felt. 'Here. Try this.' He passed her the crutch, and, reaching down, tried to help her to her feet. His hands tingled, not unpleasantly, where his skin touched hers. She sat on the ground like a tree stump, making no effort to get up.

'I told you,' she said, 'that I would do everything in my power to frustrate your plans and devices.' She looked around the grove. 'How very bland this world does look by day. And how dull.'

'Just put your weight on me, and the rest on the crutch,' he said. 'You'll have to move sometime.' He tugged on the chain and, reluctantly, the star began to get to her feet, leaning first against Tristran, and then, as if proximity to him disgusted her, on the crutch.

She gasped, then, in a hard intake of breath, and tumbled

to the grass, where she lay with her face contorted, making small noises of pain. Tristran knelt down beside her. 'What's wrong?' he asked.

Her blue eyes flashed, but they were swimming with tears. 'My leg. I can't stand on it. It must really be broken.' Her skin had gone as white as a cloud, and she was shivering.

'I'm sorry,' said Tristran, uselessly. 'I can make you a splint. I've done it for sheep. It'll be all right.' He squeezed her hand, and then he went to the brook, and dipped his handkerchief in it, and gave it to the star to wipe her forehead.

He split more fallen wood with his knife. Then he removed his jerkin, and took off his shirt, which he proceeded to tear into strips which he used to bind the sticks, as firmly as he could, about her injured leg. The star made no sounds while he did this, although, when he pulled the last knot tight, he thought he heard her whimper to herself.

'Really,' he told her, 'we ought to get you to a proper doctor. I'm not a surgeon or anything.'

'No?' she said dryly. 'You astonish me.'

He let her rest for a little, in the sun. And then he said, 'Better try again, I suppose,' and he raised her to her feet.

They left the glade at a hobble, the star leaning heavily on her crutch and on Tristran's arm, wincing at every step. And every time she winced or flinched Tristran felt guilty and awkward, but he calmed himself by thinking of Victoria Forester's grey eyes. They followed a deer path through the hazel-wood, while Tristran – who had decided that the right thing to do was to make conversation with the star – asked how long she had been a star, whether it was enjoyable to be a star and whether all stars were women, and informed her that he had always supposed stars to be, as Mrs Cherry had taught them, flaming balls of burning gas many hundreds of miles across, just like the sun only further away.

To all of these questions and statements she made no answer.

'So why did you fall?' he asked. 'Did you trip over something?'

She stopped moving, and turned, and stared at him, as if she were examining something quite unpleasant a very long way away.

'I did *not* trip,' she said at length. 'I was hit. By *this*.' She reached into her dress, and pulled out a large yellowish stone, which dangled from two lengths of silver chain. 'There's a bruise on my side where it hit me and knocked me from the sky. And now I am obliged to carry it about with me.'

'Why?'

She seemed as if she were about to answer, and then she shook her head, and her lips closed, and she said nothing at all. A stream rilled and splashed to their right, keeping pace with them. The noonday sun was overhead, and Tristran found himself getting increasingly hungry. He took the heel of the dry loaf from his bag, moistened it in the stream, and shared it out, half and half.

The star inspected the wet bread with disdain, and did not put it in her mouth.

'You'll starve,' warned Tristran.

She said nothing, just raised her chin a little higher.

They continued through the woodland, making slow progress. They were labouring up a deer path on the side of a hill, which led them over fallen trees, and which had now become so steep it threatened to tumble the stumbling star and her captor down to the bottom. 'Is there not an easier path?' asked the star, at length. 'Some kind of road, or a level clearing?'

And once the question was asked, Tristran knew the answer. 'There is a road half a mile that way,' he told her, pointing, 'and a clearing over there, beyond that thicket,' he said, turning to motion in another direction.

'You knew that?'

'Yes. No. Well, I only knew it once you asked me.'

'Let us make for the clearing,' she said, and they pushed through the thicket as best they could. It still took them the better part of an hour to reach the clearing, but the ground, when they got there, was as level and flat as a playing field. The space seemed to have been cleared with a purpose, but what that purpose was Tristran could not imagine.

In the centre of the glade, on the grass some distance from them, was an ornate golden crown, which glittered in the afternoon sunlight. It was studded with red and blue stones: *rubies and sapphires*, thought Tristran. He was about to walk over to the crown when the star touched his arm and said, 'Wait. Do you hear drums?'

He realised that he did: a low, throbbing beat, coming from all around them, near at hand and far away, which echoed through the hills. And then there came a loud crashing noise from the trees at the far side of the clearing, and a high, wordless screaming. Into the glade came a huge white horse, its flanks gashed and bloody. It charged into the middle of the clearing, and then it turned, and lowered its head, and faced its pursuer – which bounded into the clearing with a growl that made Tristran's flesh prickle. It was a lion, but it looked little enough like the lion Tristran had seen at a fair in the next village, which had been a mangy, toothless, rheumy thing. This lion was huge, the colour of sand in the late afternoon. It entered the clearing at a run, and then it stopped, and snarled at the white horse.

The horse looked terrified. Its mane was matted with sweat and blood, and its eyes were wild. Also, Tristran realised, it had a long, ivory horn jutting from the centre of its forehead. It reared up on its hind legs, whinnying and snorting, and one sharp, unshod hoof connected with the lion's shoulder, causing the lion to howl like a huge, scalded cat, and to spring backwards. Then, keeping its distance, the lion circled the wary unicorn, its golden eyes at all times fixed upon the sharp horn that was always turned toward it.

'Stop them,' whispered the star. 'They will kill each other.'

The lion growled at the unicorn. It began as a soft growl, like distant thunder, and finished as a roar that shook the trees and the rocks of the valley and the sky. Then the lion sprang and the unicorn plunged, and the glade was filled with gold and grey and red, for the lion was on the unicorn's back, claws gashing deeply into its flanks, mouth at its neck, and the unicorn was wailing and bucking and throwing itself onto its back in an effort to dislodge the great cat, flailing uselessly with its hooves and its horn in an effort to reach its tormentor.

'Please, do something. The lion will kill him,' pleaded the girl, urgently.

Tristran would have explained to her that all he could possibly hope for if he approached the raging beasts was to be skewered, and kicked, and clawed, and eaten; and he would further have explained that, should he somehow survive approaching them, there was still nothing that he could do, having with him not even the pail of water which had been the traditional method of breaking up animal fights in Wall. But by the time all these thoughts had gone through his head, Tristran was already standing in the centre of the clearing, an arm's length from the beasts. The scent of the lion was deep, animal, terrifying, and Tristran was close enough to see the beseeching expression in the unicorn's black eyes . . .

The Lion and the Unicorn were fighting for the crown, thought Tristran to himself, remembering the old nursery rhyme.

The Lion beat the Unicorn all about the town
He beat him once
He beat him twice
With all his might and main
He beat him three times over
His power to maintain

And with that, he picked up the crown from the grass; it was as heavy and as soft as lead. He walked toward the animals, talking to the lion as he had talked to the ill-tempered rams and agitated ewes in his father's fields, saying 'Here, now . . . Easy . . . Here's your crown . . .'

The lion shook the unicorn in its jaws, like a cat worrying a woolen scarf, and darted a look of pure puzzlement at Tristran.

'Hullo,' said Tristran. There were burrs and leaves in the lion's mane. He held the heavy crown out toward the great beast. 'You won. Let the unicorn go.' And he took a step closer. Then he reached out both trembling hands, and placed the crown upon the lion's head.

The lion clambered off the prone body of the unicorn and began to pad, silently, about the clearing, its head raised high. It reached the edge of the wood, where it paused for several minutes to lick its wounds with its red, red, tongue, and then, purring like an earthquake, the lion slipped away into the forest.

The star hobbled over to the injured unicorn and lowered herself to the grass, awkwardly, her broken leg splayed out by her side. She stroked its head. 'Poor, poor creature,' she said. It opened its dark eyes and stared at her, and then it laid its head upon her lap, and it closed its eyes once more.

That evening, Tristran ate the last of the hard bread for his supper, and the star ate nothing at all. She had insisted they wait beside the unicorn, and Tristran had not the heart to refuse her.

The clearing was dark, now. The sky above them was filled with the twinkling of a thousand stars. The star-woman glittered too, as if she had been brushed by the Milky Way; while the unicorn glowed gently in the darkness, like a moon seen through clouds. Tristran lay beside the huge bulk of the unicorn, feeling its warmth radiating out into the night. The star was lying on the other side of the beast. It sounded almost as if she were murmuring a song to the unicorn.

Tristran wished that he could hear her properly. The
fragments of melody he could make out were strange and
tantalizing, but she sang so quietly he could hear next to
nothing at all.

His fingers touched the chain that bound them: cold as
snow it was, and tenuous as moonlight on a millpond or the
glint of light on a trout's silver scales as it rises at dusk to
feed.

And soon he slept.

                              ***

The witch-queen drove her chariot down a forest path,
lashing the flanks of the twin white billy goats with a whip
when they flagged. She had observed the small cooking fire
burning beside the path from almost half a mile back, and
she knew from the colour of the flames that it was the fire of
one of her people, for witch-fires burn with certain unusual
hues. So she reined in her goats when she reached the
brightly painted gypsy caravan, and the cooking fire, and the
iron-haired old woman who sat beside the fire tending to the
spit over the flames on which a hare was roasting. Fat
dripped from the hare's open gut, hissing and sizzling in the
fire, which gave off the twin aromas of cooking meat and of
wood smoke.

A multicoloured bird sat by the driver's seat at the front of
the caravan, on a wooden perch. It raised its feathers and
called out in alarm when it saw the witch-queen, but it was
chained to its perch and could not leave.

'Before you says anything,' said the grey-haired woman, 'I
should tell ye that I'm just a poor old flower-seller, a
harmless old biddy who's never done nothing to no one, and
that the sight of a grand and terrifying lady such as yourself
fills me with dread and fear.'

'I will not harm you,' said the witch-queen.

The harridan screwed her eyes to slits, and looked the lady

in the red kirtle up and down. 'That's what you *says*,' she said. 'But how am I to know that it's so, a sweet old dear like me, who's all a-tremble from her toes to her water? You might be planning to rob me in the night, or worse.' And she poked the fire with a stick, so it leapt up. The smell of the cooked meat hung on the still evening air.

'I swear,' said the lady in the scarlet kirtle, 'that, by the rules and constraints of the Sisterhood to which you and I belong, by the puissance of the Lilim, and by my lips and breasts and maidenhood, that I mean you no harm, and shall treat you as if you were my own guest.'

'That's good enough for me, dearie-ducks,' said the old woman, her face breaking into a smile. 'Come and sit down. Supper'll be cooked in two shakes of a lamb's tail.'

'With good will,' said the lady in the red kirtle.

The goats snuffled and munched at the grass and the leaves beside the chariot, eyeing with distaste the tethered mules that pulled the caravan. 'Fine goats,' said the harridan. The witch-queen inclined her head and smiled modestly. The firelight glinted on the little scarlet snake wrapped as a bracelet about her wrist.

The harridan went on, 'Now, my dear, my old eyes aren't what once they were by any means, but would I be correct in supposing that one of those fine fellows started life walking on two legs, not four?'

'Such things have been heard of,' admitted the witch-queen. 'That splendid bird of yours, for example.'

'That bird gave away one of the prizes of my stock of items for sale, gave it away to a good-for-nothing, nearly twenty years ago. And afterward, the trouble she put me through scarcely bears considering. So these days, she stays a bird, unless there's work that needs doing, or the flower-stall to run; and if I could find a good strong servant, not afraid of a little hard work, why then she would stay a bird forever.'

The bird chirruped sadly upon her perch.

'They call me Mistress Semele,' said the harridan.

They called you Ditchwater Sal, when you were a young chit of a thing, thought the witch-queen, but she did not say this aloud. 'You may call me Morwanneg,' said the witch instead. It was, she reflected, almost a joke (for Morwanneg means *wave of the sea*, and her true name was long since drowned and lost beneath the cold ocean).

Mistress Semele got to her feet and made her way into the interior of the caravan, emerging with two painted wooden bowls, two wooden-handled knives, and a small pot of herbs, dried and flaked to a green powder. 'I was going to be eating with fingers on a plate of fresh leaves,' she said, handing a bowl to the lady in the scarlet kirtle. The bowl had a sunflower painted upon it, under a layer of dust. 'But I thought, well, how often does I get such fine company? So nothing but the best. Heads or tails?'

'Let it be your choice,' said her guest.

'Head, then, for you, with the luscious eyes and brains, and the crispy-crunchy ears of him. And I'll have the rump, with nothing but dull meat to nibble.' She lifted the spit off the fire as she spoke, and, using both knives so fast they seemed little more than a glitter of blades, she parted the carcass and sliced the meat from the bones, and dealt it out, fairly equitably, into each bowl. She passed the pot of herbs to her guest. 'There's no salt, my dear, but if you shake this on it will do the trick. A little basil, a little mountain thyme – my own receipt.'

The witch-queen took her portion of roasted hare, and one of the knives, and sprinkled a little of the herbs onto the dish. She speared a bite on the point of the knife and ate it with relish, while her hostess toyed with her own portion, then blew on it fastidiously, steam coming from the crisp brown meat.

'How is it?' asked the old woman.

'Perfectly palatable,' said her guest, honestly.

'It is the herbs make it so fine,' explained the harridan.

'I can taste the basil and the thyme,' said the guest,

'but there is another taste I find harder to place.'

'Ah,' said Madame Semele, and she nibbled a sliver of the meat.

'It is certainly a most uncommon taste.'

'That it is. It's a herb that grows only in Garamond, on an island in the midst of a wide lake. It is most pleasant with all manner of meats and fishes, and it reminds me in flavour a little of the leaves of fennel, with but a hint of nutmeg. The flowers of it are a most attractive shade of orange. It is good for wind and the ague, and it is, in addition, a gentle soporific, which has the curious property of causing one who tastes of it to speak nothing but the truth for several hours.'

The lady in the scarlet kirtle dropped her wooden bowl onto the ground. 'Limbus grass?' she said. 'You dared to feed me limbus grass.'

'That's how it would seem, dearie,' and the old woman cackled and hooted with delight. 'So, tell me now, Mistress Morwanneg, if that's your name, where are you a-going-of, in your fine chariot? And why do you remind me so of someone I knew once . . .? And Madame Semele forgets nothing and no one.'

'I am on my way to find a star,' said the witch-queen, 'which fell in the great woods on the other side of Mount Belly. And when I find her, I shall take my great knife and cut out her heart, while she lives, and while her heart is her own. For the heart of a living star is a sovereign remedy against all the snares of age and time. My sisters wait for me to return.'

Madame Semele hooted and hugged herself, swaying back and forth, bony fingers clutching her sides. 'The heart of a star, is it? Hee! Hee! Such a prize it will make for me. I shall taste enough of it that my youth will come back, and my hair turn from grey to golden, and my dugs swell and soften and become firm and high. Then I shall take all the heart that's left to the Great Market at Wall. Hee!'

'You shall not do this thing,' said her guest, very quietly.

'No? You are my guest, my dear. You swore your oath. You've tasted of my food. According to the laws of our Sisterhood, there is nothing you can do to harm me.'

'Oh, there are so many things I could do to harm you, Ditchwater Sal, but I shall simply point out that one who has eaten limbus grass can speak nothing but the truth for several hours afterward; and one more thing . . .' Distant lightning flickered in her words as she spoke, and the forest was hushed, as if every leaf and every tree were listening intently to what she said. 'This I say: you have stolen knowledge you did not earn, but it shall not profit you. For you shall be unable to see the star, unable to perceive it, unable to touch it, to taste it, to find it, to kill it. Even if another were to cut out its heart and give it to you, you would not know it, never know what you had in your hand. This I say. These are my words, and they are a true-speaking. And know this also: I swore, by the compact of the Sisterhood, that I would do you no harm. Had I not so sworn I would change you into a black-beetle, and I would pull your legs off, one by one, and leave you for the birds to find, for putting me to this indignity.'

Madame Semele's eyes opened wide with fright, and she stared over the flames of the fire at her guest. 'Who are you?' she said.

'When you knew me last,' said the woman in the scarlet kirtle, 'I ruled with my sisters in Carnadine, before it was lost.'

'*You*? But you are dead, long dead.'

'They have said that the Lilim were dead before now, but they have always lied. The squirrel has not yet found the acorn that will grow into the oak that will be cut to form the cradle of the babe who will grow to slay me.'

Silver flashes glittered and flared in the flames as she spoke.

'So it *is* you. And you have your youth back.' Madame

Semele sighed. 'And now I, too, shall be young again.'

The lady in the scarlet kirtle stood up then, and placed the bowl which had contained her portion of hare into the fire. 'You shall be nothing of the kind,' she said. 'Did you not hear me? A moment after I leave, you shall forget that ever you saw me. You shall forget all of this, even my curse, although the knowledge of it shall vex and irritate you, like an itch in a limb long since amputated. And may you treat your guests with more grace and respect in the future.'

The wooden bowl burst into flames then, a huge gout of flame which singed the leaves of the oak tree far above them. Madame Semele knocked the blackened bowl from the fire with a stick, and she stamped it out in the long grass. 'Whatever could have possessed me to drop the bowl into the fire?' she exclaimed aloud. 'And look, one of my nice knives, all burned up and ruined. Whatever was I a-thinking of?'

There came no answer. From further down the road came the drumming beats of something that might have been the hooves of goats, racing on into the night. Madame Semele shook her head, as if to clear it of dust and cobwebs. 'I'm getting old,' she said to the multicoloured bird who sat on its perch by the driver's seat, and who had observed everything and forgotten nothing. 'Getting old. And there's no doing anything about that.' The bird shifted uncomfortably on the perch.

A red squirrel quested, hesitating a little, into the firelight. It picked up an acorn, held it for a moment in its handlike front paws, as if it were praying. Then it ran away – to bury the acorn, and to forget it.

***

Scaithe's Ebb is a small seaport town built on granite, a town of chandlers and carpenters and sailmakers; of old sailors with missing fingers and limbs who have opened their own grog houses or spend their days in them, what is left of their hair still tarred into long queues, though the stubble on their chins has long since dusted to white. There are no whores in Scaithe's Ebb, or none that consider themselves as such, although there have always been many women who, if pressed, would describe themselves as much-married, with one husband on *this* ship here every six months, and another husband on *that* ship, back in port for a month or so every nine months.

The mathematics of the thing have always kept most folk satisfied; and if ever it disappoints and a man returns to his wife while one of her other husbands is still in occupancy, why, then there is a fight – and the grog shops to comfort the loser. The sailors do not mind the arrangement, for they know that this way there will, at the least, be one person who, at the last, will notice when they do not come back from the sea, and will mourn their loss; and their wives content themselves with the certain knowledge that their husbands are also unfaithful, for there is no competing with the sea in a man's affections, since she is both mother and mistress, and she will wash his corpse also, in time to come, wash it to coral and ivory and pearls.

So it was to Scaithe's Ebb that Lord Primus of Stormhold came one night, all dressed in black with a beard as thick and serious as one of the storks' nests in the town's chimneys. He came in a carriage drawn by four black horses and he took a room in the *Seaman's Rest* on Crook Street.

He was considered most peculiar in his needs and requests, for he brought his own food and drink into his rooms, and kept it locked in a wooden chest, which he would only open to take himself an apple, or a wedge of cheese, or a cup of pepper-wine. His was the topmost room in the *Seaman's Rest*, a high and spindly building, built on a rocky outcrop to facilitate smuggling.

He bribed a number of the local street urchins to report to him the moment they saw any fellow they did not know come to town, by land or sea; in particular, they were to look for a very tall, angular, dark-haired fellow, with a thin hungry face, and blank eyes.

'Primus is certainly learning caution,' said Secundus to his five other dead brothers.

'Well, you know what they say,' whispered Quintus, in the wistful tones of the dead, which sounded, on that day, like the lapping of distant waves upon the shingle, 'a man who is tired of looking over his shoulder for Septimus is tired of life.'

In the mornings, Primus would talk to the sea captains with ships in Scaithe's Ebb, buying them grog liberally, but neither drinking nor eating with them. In the afternoon he would inspect the ships in the docks.

Soon the gossips of Scaithe's Ebb (and there were many) had the gist and juice of it all: the bearded gentleman was to be taking ship to the East. And this tale was soon chased by another, that he would be sailing out on the *Heart of a Dream* under Captain Yann, a black-trimmed ship with its decks painted crimson red, of more or less savoury reputation (by which I mean that it was generally held that she kept her piracies for distant waters) and this would be happening as soon as he gave the word.

'Good master!' said a street urchin to Lord Primus. 'There's a man in town, come by land. He lodges with Mistress Pettier. He is thin and crowlike, and I saw him in the *Ocean's Roar*, buying grog for every man in the room. He says he is a distressed seafaring man, seeking a berth.'

Primus patted the boy's filthy head and handed him a coin. Then he returned to his preparations, and that afternoon it was announced that the *Heart of a Dream* would leave harbour in three short days.

The day before the *Heart of a Dream* was to set sail, Primus was seen to sell his coach and four horses to the stableman on Wardle Street, after which he walked down to the quay, dispensing small coins to the urchins. He entered his cabin in the *Heart of a Dream* and gave strict orders that

none was to disturb him, for any reason, good or bad, until
they were at least a week out of port.

That evening an unfortunate accident befell an able
seaman who had crewed the rigging on the *Heart of a Dream*.
He fell, when drunk, on the slippery cobblestones of
Revenue Street, and broke his hip. Luckily there was a
replacement at the ready: the very sailor with whom he had
been drinking that evening, and to whom the injured man
had been persuaded to demonstrate a particularly
complicated hornpipe step on the wet cobbles. And this
sailor, tall, dark and crowlike, marked his ship's papers with
a circle that night and was on deck at dawn when the ship
sailed out of the harbour, in the morning mist. The *Heart of
a Dream* sailed east.

Lord Primus of Stormhold, his beard freshly shaven,
watched it sail from the cliff top until it was lost to view.
Then he walked down to Wardle Street, where he returned
the stableman's money and something more besides, and he
rode off on the coast road toward the west, in a dark coach
pulled by four black horses.

***

It was an obvious solution. After all, the unicorn had been
ambling hugely behind them for most of the morning,
occasionally nudging the star's shoulder with its big
forehead. The wounds on its dappled flanks, which had
blossomed like red flowers under the lion's claws the day
before, were now dried to brown and scabbed over.

The star limped and hobbled and stumbled, and Tristran
walked beside her, cold chain binding wrist to wrist.

On the one hand, Tristran felt there was something almost
sacrilegious about the idea of riding the unicorn: it was not
a horse, did not subscribe to any of the ancient pacts
between Man and Horse. There was a wildness in its black
eyes, and a twisting spring to its step which was dangerous

and untamed. On the other hand, Tristran had begun to feel, in a way that he could not articulate, that the unicorn cared about the star, and wished to help her. So he said, 'Look, I know all that stuff about frustrating my plans every step of the way, but if the unicorn is willing, perhaps it would carry you on its back, for a little way.'

The star said nothing.

'Well?'

She shrugged.

Tristran turned to the unicorn, stared into its pool-black eyes. 'Can you understand me?' he asked. It said nothing. He had hoped it would nod its head or stamp a hoof, like a trained horse he had once seen on the village green when he was younger. But it simply stared. 'Will you carry the lady? Please?'

The beast said not a word, nor did it nod or stamp. But it walked to the star, and it knelt down at her feet.

Tristran helped the star onto the unicorn's back. She grasped its tangled mane with both hands and sat sidesaddle upon it, her broken leg sticking out. And that was how they travelled for some hours.

Tristran walked along beside them, carrying her crutch over his shoulder, with his bag dangling from the end. He found it as hard to travel with the star riding the unicorn as it had been before. Then he had been forced to walk slowly, trying to keep pace with the star's limping hobble – now he was hurrying to keep up with the unicorn, nervous lest the unicorn should get too far ahead and the chain that linked them both should pull the star from the beast's back. His stomach rumbled, as he walked. He was painfully aware how hungry he was; soon Tristran began to think of himself as nothing more than hunger, thinly surrounded by flesh, and, as fast as he could, walking, walking . . .

He stumbled and knew that he was going to fall.

'Please, stop,' he gasped.

The unicorn slowed, and stopped. The star looked down

at him. Then she made a face, and shook her head. 'You had better come up here, too,' she said. 'If the unicorn will let you. Otherwise you'll just faint or something, and drag me onto the ground with you. And we need to go somewhere so that you can get food.'

Tristran nodded, gratefully.

The unicorn appeared to offer no opposition, waiting, passively, so Tristran attempted to clamber up onto it. It was like climbing a sheer wall, and as fruitless. Eventually Tristran led the animal over to a beech tree that had been uprooted several years before by a storm, or a high wind, or an irritable giant, and, holding his bag and the star's crutch, he scrambled up the roots onto the trunk, and from there onto the back of the unicorn.

'There is a village on the other side of that hill,' said Tristran. 'I expect that we can find something to eat when we get there.' He patted the unicorn's flanks with his free hand. The beast began to walk. Tristran moved his hand to the star's waist, to steady himself. He could feel the silken texture of her thin dress, and beneath that, the thick chain of the topaz about her waist.

Riding a unicorn was not like riding a horse: it did not move like a horse; it was a wilder ride, and a stranger one. The unicorn waited until Tristran and the star were comfortable upon its back, and then, slowly and easily, it began to put on speed.

The trees surged and leapt past them. The star leaned forward, her fingers tangled into the unicorn's mane; Tristran – his hunger forgotten in his fear – gripped the sides of the unicorn with his knees, and simply prayed that he would not be knocked to the ground by a stray branch. Soon he found he was beginning to enjoy the experience. There is something about riding a unicorn, for those people who still can, which is unlike any other experience: exhilarating and intoxicating and fine.

The sun was setting when they reached the outskirts of

the village. In a rolling meadow, beneath an oak tree, the unicorn came to a skittish halt and would go no further. Tristran dismounted, and landed with a bump on the grass of the meadow. His rump felt sore, but, with the star looking down at him, uncomplaining, he dared not rub it.

'Are *you* hungry?' he asked the star.

She said nothing.

'Look,' he said, 'I'm starving. Perfectly famished. I don't know if you – if stars – eat, or *what* they eat. But I won't have you starving yourself.' He looked up at her, questioning. She stared down at him, first impassively, then, in a trice, her blue eyes filled with tears. She raised a hand to her face and wiped away the tears, leaving a smudge of mud on her cheeks.

'We eat only darkness,' she said, 'and we drink only light. So I'm nuh-not hungry. I'm lonely and scared and cold and muh-miserable and cuh-captured but I'm nuh-not hungry.'

'Don't cry,' said Tristran. 'Look, I'll go into the village and get some food. You just wait here. The unicorn will protect you, if anyone comes.' He reached up and gently lifted her down from the unicorn's back. The unicorn shook its mane, then began to crop the grass of the meadow, contentedly.

The star sniffed, 'Wait here?' she asked, holding up the chain that joined them.

'Oh,' said Tristran. 'Give me your hand.'

She reached her hand out to him. He fumbled with the chain to undo it, but it would not undo. 'Hmm,' said Tristran. He tugged at the chain around his own wrist, but it, too, held fast. 'It looks,' he said, 'as if I'm as tied to you as you are to me.'

The star threw her hair back, closed her eyes, and sighed deeply. And then, opening her eyes, once again self-possessed, she said, 'Perhaps there's a magic word or something.'

'I don't know any magic words,' said Tristran. He held the chain up. It glittered red and purple in the light of the setting

sun. 'Please?' he said. There was a ripple in the fabric of the
chain, and he slid his hand out of it.

'Here you go,' he said, passing the star the other end of
the chain that had bound her. 'I'll try not to be too long.
And if any of the fair folk sing their silly songs at you, for
heaven's sake, don't throw your crutch at them. They'll
only steal it.'

'I won't,' she said.

'I'll have to trust you, on your honour as a star, not to run
away,' he said.

She touched her splinted leg. 'I will do no running for
quite some time,' she said, pointedly. And with that Tristran
had to content himself.

He walked the last half a mile into the village. It had no
inn, being far off the beaten track for travellers, but the
portly old woman who explained this to him then insisted he
accompany her to her cottage, where she pressed upon him
a wooden bowlful of barley porridge with carrots in it, and a
mug of small beer. He exchanged his cambric handkerchief
for a bottle of elderflower cordial, a round of green cheese
and a number of unfamiliar fruits: they were soft and fuzzy,
like apricots, but were the purple-blue of grapes, and they
smelled a little like ripe pears; also the woman gave him a
small bale of hay, for the unicorn.

He walked back to the meadow where he had left them,
munching on a piece of the fruit, which was juicy, and
chewy and quite sweet. He wondered if the star would like
to try one, whether she would like it if she did. He hoped
that she would be pleased with what he had brought her.

At first, Tristran thought that he must have made a
mistake, and that he had lost his way in the moonlight. No:
that was the same oak tree, the one beneath which the star
had been sitting.

'Hello?' he called. Glow-worms and fireflies glittered green
and yellow in the hedgerows and in the branches of trees.
There came no reply, and Tristran felt a sick, stupid feeling

in the pit of his stomach. 'Hello?' he called. He stopped calling, then, because there was no one to answer.

He dropped the bale of hay, and then he kicked it.

She was to the southwest of him, moving faster than he could walk. He followed after her in the bright moonlight. Inside, he felt numbed and foolish; stung by a pang of guilt and shame and regret. He should not have loosed her chain, he should have tied it to a tree; he should have forced the star to go with him into the village. This went through his head as he walked; but another voice spoke to him also, pointing out that if he had not unchained her then, he would have done it sometime soon, and she would have run from him then.

He wondered if he would ever see the star again, and he stumbled over roots as the way led him between old trees, into the deep woods. The moonlight slowly vanished beneath the thick canopy of leaves, and after stumbling vainly in the dark for a short while, he laid himself down beneath a tree, rested his head on his bag, and closed his eyes, and felt sorry for himself until he fell asleep.

***

On a rocky mountain pass, on the southernmost slopes of Mount Belly, the witch-queen reined in her goat-drawn chariot and stopped and sniffed the chilly air.

The myriad stars hung cold in the sky above her.

Her red, red lips curved up into a smile of such beauty, such brilliance, such pure and perfect happiness that it would have frozen your blood in your veins to have seen it. 'There,' she said. 'She is coming to me.'

And the wind of the mountain pass howled about her triumphantly, as if in answer.

***

Primus sat beside the embers of his fire and he shivered beneath his thick black robe. One of the black stallions, waking or dreaming, whinnied and snorted, and then rested once more. Primus's face felt strangely cold; he missed his thick beard. With a stick he pushed a clay ball from the embers. He spat on his hands, then he split open the hot clay and smelled the sweet flesh of the hedgehog, which had cooked, slowly, in the embers, as he had slept.

He ate his breakfast meticulously, spitting the tiny bones into the fire circle once he had chewed the meat from them. He washed the hedgehog down with a lump of hard cheese and a slightly vinegary white wine.

Once he had eaten, he wiped his hands upon his robe and then he cast the runes to find the topaz stone which conferred the lordship of the crag towns and the vast estates of the Stormhold. He cast them, then he stared, puzzled, at the small, square, red granite tiles. He picked them up once more, shook them in his long-fingered hands, dropped them onto the ground and stared at them again. Then Primus spat into the embers, which hissed lazily. He swept the tiles up and dropped them into the pouch at his belt.

'It is moving faster, further,' said Primus to himself.

He pissed on the embers of the fire, for he was in wild country, and there were bandits and hobgoblins and worse in those lands, and he had no desire to alert them to his presence. Then, he hitched the horses to the carriage and climbed into the driver's seat, and drove them towards the forest, to the west, and to the mountain range beyond.

***

The girl held tight to the unicorn's neck as it tumbled headlong through the dark forest.

There was no moonlight between the trees, but the unicorn glimmered and shone with pale light, like the moon, while the girl herself glittered and glowed as if she trailed a dust of lights. And, as she passed through the trees, it might have appeared to a distant observer that she seemed to twinkle, on and off and off and on, like a tiny star.

Chapter Six

What the Tree Said

T ristran Thorn was dreaming.

He was in an apple tree, staring through a window at Victoria Forester, who was getting undressed. As she removed her dress, revealing a healthy expanse of petticoat, Tristran felt the branch begin to give way beneath his feet, and then he was tumbling down through the air in the moonlight . . .

He was falling into the moon.

And the moon was talking to him: *Please*, whispered the moon, in a voice that reminded him a little of his mother's, *protect her. Protect my child. They mean her harm. I have done all I can.* And the moon would have told him more, and perhaps she did, but the moon became the glimmer of moonlight on water far below him, and then he became aware of a small spider walking across his face, and of a crick in his neck, and he raised a hand and brushed the spider carefully from his cheek, and the morning sun was in his eyes and the world was gold and green.

'You were dreaming,' said a young woman's voice from somewhere above him. The voice was gentle, and oddly

accented. He could hear leaves rustle in the copper beech
tree overhead.

'Yes,' he said, to whoever was in the tree, 'I was dreaming.'

'I had a dream last night, too,' said the voice. 'In my dream,
I looked up and I could see the whole forest, and something
huge was moving through it. And it got closer, and closer,
and I knew what it was.' She stopped talking abruptly.

'What was it?' asked Tristran.

'Everything,' she said. 'It was Pan. When I was very young,
somebody – maybe it was a squirrel, they talk so much, or a
magpie, or maybe a fishie – told me that Pan owned all this
forest. Well, not *owned* owned. Not like he would sell the
forest to someone else, or put a wall all around it—'

'Or cut down the trees,' said Tristran, helpfully. There was
a silence. He wondered where the girl had gone. 'Hello?' he
said. 'Hello?'

There was another rustle of leaves from above him.

'You shouldn't say things like that,' she said.

'Sorry,' said Tristran, not entirely sure what he was apolo-
gising for. 'But you were telling me that Pan owned the
forest . . .'

'Of course he does,' said the voice. 'It's not hard to own
something. Or everything. You just have to know that it's
yours, and then be willing to let it go. Pan owns this forest,
like that. And in my dream he came over to me. You were in
my dream, too, leading a sad girl by a chain. She was a very
sad, sad girl. Pan told me to help you.'

'Me?'

'And it made me feel all warm and tingly and squishy
inside, from the tips of my leaves to the end of my roots. So
I woke up, and there you were, fast asleep with your head by
my trunk, snoring like a pigwiggin.'

Tristran scratched his nose. He stopped looking for a
woman in the branches of the copper beech tree above him,
and looked instead at the tree itself. 'You are a tree,' said
Tristran, putting his thoughts into words.

'I didn't always used to be a tree,' said the voice in the rustling of the copper beech leaves. 'A magician made me a tree.'

'What were you before?' asked Tristran.

'Do you think he likes me?'

'Who?'

'Pan. If you were the Lord of the Forest, you wouldn't give a job to someone, tell them to give all possible aid and succour, unless you liked them, would you?'

'Well . . .' said Tristran, but before he had decided on the politic answer, the tree had already said, 'A nymph. I was a wood-nymph. But I got pursued by a prince, not a nice prince, the other kind, and, well, you'd think a prince, even the wrong kind, would understand about boundaries, wouldn't you?'

'You would?'

'Exactly what I think. But he didn't, so I did a bit of invoking while I was running, and – *ba-boom*! – tree. What do you think?'

'Well,' said Tristran. 'I do not know what you were like as a wood-nymph, madam, but you are a magnificent tree.'

The tree made no immediate reply, but her leaves rustled prettily. 'I was pretty cute as a nymph, too,' she admitted, coyly.

'What kind of aid and succour, exactly?' asked Tristran. 'Not that I am grumbling. I mean, right now I need all the aid and succour I can get. But a tree is not necessarily the obvious place to look for it. You cannot come with me, or feed me, or bring the star here, or send us back to Wall to see my true love. I am certain you would do a remarkable job of keeping off the rain, were it to rain, but it is not, at present, raining . . .'

The tree rustled. 'Why don't you tell me your story so far,' said the tree, 'and let me be the best judge of whether or not I can be of help.'

Tristran began to protest. He could feel the star moving

further and further away from him, at the speed of a
cantering unicorn, and if there was one thing he did not
have time for, it was the recitation of the adventures of his
life to date. But then it occurred to him that any progress he
had made on his quest so far he had made by accepting the
help that had been offered to him. So he sat on the
woodland floor and he told the copper beech everything he
could think of: about his love, pure and true, for Victoria
Forester; his promise to bring her a fallen star – not any
fallen star, but the one they had seen, together, from the top
of Dyties Hill; and of his journey into Faerie. He told the tree
of his journeyings, of the little hairy man and of the small
fair folk who stole his bowler hat; he told her of the magic
candle, and his walk across the leagues to the star's side in
the glade, and of the lion and the unicorn, and of how he
had lost the star.

He finished his story, and there was silence. The copper
leaves on the tree shivered, softly, as if in a gentle wind,
and then harder, as if a storm were coming. And then the
leaves formed a fierce, low voice, which said, 'If you had
kept her chained, and she had escaped her chains, then
there is no power on earth or sky could ever make me help
you, not if Great Pan or Lady Sylvia herself were to plead or
implore me. But you unchained her, and for that I will help
you.'

'Thank you,' said Tristran.

'I will tell you three true things. Two of them I will tell you
now, and the last is for when you need it most. You will have
to judge for yourself when that will be.

'First, the star is in great danger. What occurs in the midst
of a wood is soon known at its furthest borders, and the
trees talk to the wind, and the wind passes the word along
to the next wood it comes to. There are forces that mean her
harm, and worse than harm. You must find her, and protect
her.

'Secondly, there is a path through the forest, off past that fir tree (and I could tell you things about that fir tree that would make a boulder blush), and in a few minutes a carriage will be coming down that path. Hurry, and you will not miss it.

'And thirdly, hold out your hands.'

Tristran held out his hands. From high above him a copper-coloured leaf came falling slowly, spinning and gliding and tumbling down. It landed neatly in the palm of his right hand.

'There,' said the tree. 'Keep it safe. And listen to it, when you need it most. Now,' she told him, 'the coach is nearly here. Run! Run!'

Tristran picked up his bag and he ran, fumbling the leaf into the pocket of his tunic as he did so. He could hear hoofbeats through the glade, coming closer and closer. He knew that he could not reach it in time, despaired of reaching it, but still he ran faster, until all he could hear was his heart pounding in his chest and his ears, and the hiss of air as he pulled it into his lungs. He scrambled and dashed through the bracken and made it to the path as the carriage came down the track.

It was a black coach drawn by four night-black horses, driven by a pale fellow in a long black robe. It was twenty paces from Tristran. He stood there, gulping breath, and then he tried to call out, but his throat was dry, and his wind was gone, and his voice came from him in a dry sort of croaking whisper. He tried to shout, and simply wheezed.

The carriage passed him by without slowing.

Tristran sat on the ground and caught his breath. Then, afraid for the star, he got back to his feet and walked, as fast as he could manage, along the forest path. He had not walked for more than ten minutes when he came upon the black coach. A huge branch, itself as big as some trees, had fallen from an oak tree onto the path directly in front of the horses, and the driver, who was also the coach's sole occupant, was endeavouring to lift it out of the way.

'Damnedest thing,' said the coachman, who wore a long black robe and who Tristran estimated to be in his late forties, 'there was no wind, no storm. It simply fell. Terrified the horses.' His voice was deep and booming.

Tristran and the driver unhitched the horses, and roped them to the oak branch. Then the two men pushed, and the four horses pulled, and together they dragged the branch to the side of the track. Tristran said a silent *thank you* to the oak tree whose branch had fallen, to the copper beech and to Pan of the forests, and then he asked the driver if he would give him a ride through the forest.

'I do not take passengers,' said the driver, rubbing his bearded chin.

'Of course,' said Tristran. 'But without me you would still be stuck here. Surely Providence sent you to me, just as Providence sent me to you. I will not take you out of your path, and there may again come a time when you are glad of another pair of hands.'

The coach driver looked Tristran over from his head to his feet. Then he reached into the velvet bag that hung from his belt, and removed a handful of square red granite tiles.

'Pick one,' he said to Tristran.

Tristran picked a stone tile, and showed the symbol carved upon it to the man. 'Hmm,' was all the driver said. 'Now pick another.' Tristran did so. 'And another.' The man rubbed his chin once more. 'Yes, you can come with me,' he said. 'The runes seem certain of that. Although there will be danger. But perhaps there *will* be more fallen branches to move. You can sit up front, if you wish, on the driver's seat beside me, and keep me company.'

It was a peculiar thing, observed Tristran as he climbed up into the driver's seat, but the first time he had glanced into the interior of the coach he had fancied that he saw five pale gentlemen, all in grey, staring sadly out at him. But the next time he had looked inside, nobody had been there at all.

The carriage rattled and pounded over the grassy track beneath a golden-green canopy of leaves. Tristran worried about the star. She might be ill-tempered, he thought, but it was with a certain amount of justification, after all. He hoped that she could stay out of trouble until he caught up with her.

**

It was sometimes said that the grey-and-black mountain range which ran like a spine north to south down that part of Faerie had once been a giant, who grew so huge and so heavy that, one day, worn out from the sheer effort of moving and living, he had stretched out on the plain and fallen into a sleep so profound that centuries passed between heartbeats. This would have been a long time ago, if it ever happened, in the First Age of the world, when all was stone and fire, water and wind, and there were few left alive to put the lie to it if it was not true. Still, true or not, they called the four great mountains of the range Mount Head, Mount Shoulder, Mount Belly and Mount Knees, and the foothills to the south were known as the Feet. There were passes through the mountains, one between the head and the shoulders, where the neck would have been, and one immediately to the south of Mount Belly.

They were wild mountains, inhabited by wild creatures: slate-coloured trolls, hairy wild-men, strayed wodwos, mountain goats and mining gnomes, hermits and exiles and the occasional peak-witch. This was not one of the really high mountain ranges of Faerie, such as Mount Huon, on the top of which is the Stormhold but it was a hard range for lone travellers to cross nonetheless.

The witch-queen had crossed the pass south of Mount Belly in a couple of days, and now waited at the opening of the pass. Her goats were tethered to a thorn bush, which they chewed without enthusiasm. She sat on the side of the unhitched chariot and sharpened her knives with a whet-stone.

The knives were old things: the hilts were made of bone, while the blades were chipped, volcanic glass, black as jet, with white snowflake-shapes frozen forever into the obsidian. There were two knives: the smaller, a hatchet-bladed cleaver, heavy and hard, for cutting through the rib cage, for jointing and segmenting; the other a long, dagger-like blade, for cutting out the heart. When the knives were so sharp that she could have drawn either blade across your throat, and you would never have felt more than the touch of the lightest hair, as the spreading warmth of your life's blood made a quiet escape, the witch-queen put them away and commenced her preparations.

She walked over to the goats and whispered a word of power to each of them.

Where the goats had been stood a man with a white chin-beard, and a boyish, dull-eyed young woman. They said nothing.

She crouched beside her chariot, and whispered several words to it. The chariot did nothing, and the witch-woman stamped her foot on the rock.

'I am getting old,' she said to her two servants. They said nothing in reply, gave no indication that they even understood her. 'Things inanimate have always been more difficult to change than things animate. Their souls are older and stupider and harder to persuade. If I but had my true youth again . . . why, in the dawn of the world I could transform mountains into seas and clouds into palaces. I could populate cities with the pebbles on the shingle. If I were young again . . .'

She sighed and raised a hand: a blue flame flickered about her fingers for a moment, and then, as she lowered her hand and bent down to touch her chariot, the fire vanished.

She stood up straight. There were streaks of grey now in

her raven-black hair, and dark pouches beneath her eyes; but the chariot was gone, and she stood in front of a small inn at the edge of the mountain pass.

Far away the thunder rumbled, quietly, and lightning flickered in the distance.

The inn sign swung and creaked in the wind. There was a picture of a chariot painted upon it.

'You two,' said the witch-woman, 'inside. She is riding this way, and she will have to come through this pass. Now I simply have to ensure that she will come inside. *You*,' she said to the man with the white chin-beard, 'are Billy, the owner of this tavern. I shall be your wife, and *this*,' pointing to the dull-eyed girl, who had once been Brevis, 'is our daughter, the pot-maid.'

Another crash of thunder echoed down from the mountain peaks, louder than before.

'It will rain soon,' said the witch-woman. 'Let us prepare the fire.'

* * *

Tristran could feel the star ahead of them, moving steadily onward. He felt as if he were gaining ground upon her.

And, to his relief, the black carriage continued to follow the star's path. Once, when the road diverged, Tristran was concerned that they might take the wrong fork. He was ready to leave the coach and travel on alone, if that should happen.

His companion reined in the horses, clambered down from the driver's seat, and took out his runes. Then, his consultation complete, he climbed back up, and took the carriage down the left-hand fork.

'If it is not too forward of me to enquire,' said Tristran, 'might I ask what it is that you are in search of?'

'My destiny,' said the man, after a short pause. 'My right to rule. And you?'

'There's a young lady that I have offended with my

behaviour,' said Tristran. 'I wish to make amends.' As he said it, he knew it to be true.

The driver grunted.

The forest canopy was thinning rapidly. Trees became sparser, and Tristran stared up at the mountains in front of them, and he gasped. 'Such mountains!' he said.

'When you are older,' said his companion, 'you must visit my citadel, high on the crags of Mount Huon. Now *that* is a mountain, and from there we can look down upon mountains next to which *these*,' and he gestured toward the heights of Mount Belly, ahead of them, 'are the merest foothills.'

'Truth to tell,' said Tristran, 'I hope to spend the rest of my life as a sheep farmer in the village of Wall, for I have now had as much excitement as any man could rightly need, what with candles and trees and the young lady and the unicorn. But I take the invitation in the spirit in which it was given, and thank you for it. If ever you visit Wall then you must come to my house, and I shall give you woolen clothes and sheep-cheese, and all the mutton stew you can eat.'

'You are far too kind,' said the driver. The path was easier now, made of crushed gravel and graded rocks, and he cracked his whip to urge the four black stallions on faster. 'You saw a unicorn, you say?'

Tristran was about to tell his companion all about the encounter with the unicorn, but he thought better of it, and simply said, 'He was a most noble beast.'

'The unicorns are the moon's creatures,' said the driver. 'I have never seen one. But it is said that they serve the moon and do her bidding. We shall reach the mountains by tomorrow evening. I shall call a halt at sunset tonight. If you wish, you may sleep inside the coach; I, myself, shall sleep beside the fire.' There was no change in his tone of voice, but Tristran knew, with a certainty that was both sudden and shocking in its intensity, that the man was scared of something, frightened to the depths of his soul.

Lightning flickered on the mountaintops that night. Tristran slept on the leather seat of the coach, his head on a sack of oats; he dreamed of ghosts, and of the moon and stars.

The rain began at dawn, abruptly, as if the sky had turned to water. Low, grey clouds hid the mountains from sight. In the driving rain Tristran and the coach driver hitched the horses to the carriage and set off. It was all uphill, now, and the horses went no faster than a walk.

'You could go inside,' said the driver. 'No point in us both getting wet.' They had put on one-piece oilskins they had found beneath the driver's seat.

'It would be hard for me to be wetter,' said Tristran, 'without my first leaping into a river. I shall stay here. Two pairs of eyes and two pairs of hands may well be the saving of us.'

His companion grunted. He wiped the rain from his eyes and mouth with a cold wet hand, and then he said, 'You're a fool, boy. But I appreciate it.' He transferred the reins to his left hand, and extended his right hand. 'I am known as Primus. The Lord Primus.'

'Tristran. Tristran Thorn,' he said, feeling that the man had, somehow, earned the right to know his true name.

They shook hands. The rain fell harder. The horses slowed to the slowest walk as the path became a stream, and the heavy rain cut off all vision as effectively as the thickest fog.

'There is a man,' said the Lord Primus, shouting to be heard now over the rain, the wind whipping the words from his lips. 'He is tall, looks a little like me, but thinner, more crowlike. His eyes seem innocent and dull, but there is death in them. He is called Septimus, for he was the seventh boy-child our father spawned. If ever you see him, run and hide. His business is with me. But he will not hesitate to kill you if you stand in his way, or, perhaps, to make you his instrument with which to kill me.'

A wild gust of wind drove a tankardful of rainwater down Tristran's neck.

'He sounds a most dangerous man,' said Tristran.

'He is the most dangerous man you will ever meet.'

Tristran peered silently into the rain, and the gathering darkness. It was becoming harder to see the road. Primus spoke again, saying, 'If you ask me, there is something unnatural about this storm.'

'Unnatural?'

'Or more-than-natural; super-natural, if you will. I hope there is an inn along the way. The horses need a rest, and I could do with a dry bed and a warm fire. And a good meal.'

Tristran shouted his agreement. They sat together, getting wetter. Tristran thought about the star and the unicorn. She would be cold by now, and wet. He worried about her broken leg, and thought about how saddle sore she must be. It was all his fault. He felt wretched.

'I am the most miserable person who ever lived,' he said to the Lord Primus, when they stopped to feed the horses feedbags of damp oats.

'You are young, and in love,' said Primus. 'Every young man in your position is the most miserable young man who ever lived.'

Tristran wondered how Lord Primus could have divined the existence of Victoria Forester. He imagined himself recounting his adventures to her, back at Wall, in front of a blazing parlour fire; but somehow all of his tales seemed a little flat.

Dusk seemed to have started at dawn that day, and now the sky was almost black. Their path continued to climb. The rain would let up for moments, and then redouble, falling harder than ever.

'Is that a light over there?' asked Tristran.

'I cannot see anything. Maybe it was fool's fire, or lightning . . .' said Primus. And then they gained a bend in the road, and he said, 'I was wrong. That *is* a light. Well-spotted, young 'un. But there are bad things in these mountains. We must only hope that they are friendly.'

The horses put on a fresh burst of speed, now that their destination was in sight. A flash of lightning revealed the mountains, rising steeply up on either side of them.

'We're in luck!' said Primus, his bass voice booming like thunder. 'It's an inn!'

Chapter Seven

'At the Sign of the Chariot'

The star had been soaked to the skin when she arrived at the pass, sad and shivering. She was worried about the unicorn; they had found no food for it on the last day's journey, as the grasses and ferns of the forest had been replaced by grey rocks and stunted thorn bushes. The unicorn's unshod hooves were not meant for the rocky road, nor was its back meant to carry riders, and its pace became slower and slower.

As they travelled, the star cursed the day she had fallen to this wet, unfriendly world. It had seemed so gentle and welcoming when seen from high in the sky. That was before. Now, she hated everything about it, except the unicorn; and, saddle sore and uncomfortable, she would have happily spent time away from the unicorn.

After a day of pelting rain, the lights of the inn were the most welcoming sight she had seen in her time on the Earth. *'Watch your step, watch your step,'* pattered the raindrops on the stone. The unicorn stopped, fifty yards from the inn, and would approach no closer. The door to the inn was opened, flooding the grey world with warm yellow light.

'Hello there, dearie,' called a welcoming voice from the open doorway.

The star stroked the unicorn's wet neck and spoke softly to the animal, but it made no move, stood there frozen in the light of the inn like a pale ghost.

'Will you be coming in, dearie? Or will you be stopping out there in the rain?' The woman's friendly voice warmed the star, soothed her: just the right mixture of practicality and concern. 'We can get you food, if it's food you're after. There's a fire blazing in the hearth, and enough hot water for a tub that'll melt the chill from your bones.'

'I . . . I will need help coming in . . .' said the star. 'My leg . . .'

'Ach, poor mite,' said the woman. 'I'll have my husband Billy carry you inside. There's hay and fresh water in the stables, for your beast.'

The unicorn looked about wildly as the woman approached. 'There, there, dearie. I won't be coming too close. After all, it's been many a long year since I was maiden enough to touch a unicorn, and many a long year since such a one was seen in *these* parts . . .'

Nervously, the unicorn followed the woman into the stables, keeping its distance from her. It walked along the stable to the furthest stall, where it lay down in the dry straw, and the star scrambled off its back, dripping and miserable.

Billy turned out to be a white-bearded, gruff sort of fellow. He said little, but carried the star into the inn, and put her down on a three-legged stool in front of a crackling log fire.

'Poor dear,' said the innkeeper's wife, who had followed them inside. 'Look at you, wet as a water-nixie, look at the puddle under you, and your lovely dress, oh the state of it, you must be soaked to the bone . . .' And, sending her husband away, she helped the star remove her dripping wet dress, which she placed on a hook near the fire, where each drip hissed and fizzed when it fell to the hot bricks of the hearth.

There was a tin tub in front of the fire, and the innkeeper's wife put up a paper screen around it. 'How d'you like your baths?' she asked, solicitously, 'warm, hot, or boil-a-lobster?'

'I do not know,' said the star, naked but for the topaz-stone on the silver chain about her waist, her head all in a whirl at the strange turn that events had taken, 'for I have never had a bath before.'

'Never had one?' The innkeeper's wife looked astonished. 'Why, you poor duck; well, we won't make it *too* hot, then. Call me if you need another copperful of water, I've got some going over the kitchen fire; and when you're done with the bath, I'll bring you some mulled wine, and some sweet-roasted turnips.'

And, before the star could protest that she neither ate nor drank, the woman had bustled off, leaving the star sitting in the tin tub, her broken leg in its splints sticking out of the water and resting on the three-legged stool. Initially the water was indeed too hot, but as she became used to the heat she relaxed, and was, for the first time since she had tumbled from the sky, utterly happy.

'There's a love,' said the innkeeper's wife, returning. 'How are you feeling now?'

'Much, much better, thank you,' said the star.

'And your heart? How does your heart feel?' asked the woman.

'My heart?' It was a strange question, but the woman seemed genuinely concerned. 'It feels happier. More easy. Less troubled.'

'Good. That's good. Let us get it burning high and hot within you, eh? Burning bright inside you.'

'I am sure that under your care my heart shall blaze and burn with happiness,' said the star.

The innkeeper's wife leaned over and chucked the star under the chin. 'There's a pet, such a duck it is, the fine things it says.' And the woman smiled indulgently, and ran a hand through her grey-streaked hair. She hung a thick towelling robe on the edge of the screen. 'This is for you to wear when you are done with your bath – oh no, not to hurry, ducks – it'll be nice and warm for you, and your pretty dress will still be damp for a while now. Just give us a shout when you want to hop out of the tub and I'll come and give you a hand.' Then she leaned over, and touched the star's chest, between her breasts, with one cold finger. And she smiled. 'A good strong heart,' she said.

There *were* good people on this benighted world, the star decided, warmed and contented. Outside the rain and the wind pattered and howled through the mountain pass, but in the inn, at the Sign of the Chariot, all was warm and comfortable.

Eventually the innkeeper's wife, assisted by her dull-faced daughter, helped the star out of her bath. The firelight glinted on the topaz set in silver which the star wore on a knotted silver chain about her waist, until the topaz, and the star's body, vanished beneath the thick towelling of her robe.

'Now my sweet,' said the innkeeper's wife, 'you come over here and make yourself comfortable.' She helped the star over to a long wooden table, at the head of which were laid a cleaver and a knife, both of them with hilts of bone and blades of dark glass. Leaning and limping, the star made it to the table, and sat down at the bench beside it.

Outside there was a gust of wind, and the fire flared up green and blue and white. Then a deep voice boomed from outside the inn, over the howl of the elements. 'Service! Food! Wine! Fire! Where is the stableboy?'

Billy the innkeeper and his daughter made no move, but only looked at the woman in the red dress as if for instructions. She pursed her lips. And then she said, 'It can wait. For a little. After all, you are not going anywhere, my dearie?' This last to the star. 'Not on that leg of yours, and not until the rain lets up, eh?'

'I appreciate your hospitality more than I can say,' said the star, simply and with feeling.

'Of course you do,' said the woman in the red dress, and her fidgeting fingers brushed the black knives impatiently, as if there were something she could not wait to be doing. 'Plenty of time when these nuisances have gone, eh?'

* * *

The light of the inn was the happiest and best thing Tristran had seen on his journey through Faerie. While Primus bellowed for assistance, Tristran unhitched the exhausted horses, and led them one by one into the stables on the side of the inn. There was a white horse asleep in the furthest stall, but Tristran was too busy to pause to inspect it.

He knew – somewhere in the odd place inside him that knew directions and distances of things he had never seen and the places he had never been – that the star was close at hand, and this comforted him, and it also made him nervous. He knew that the horses were more exhausted and more hungry than he was. His dinner – and thus, he suspected, his confrontation with the star – could wait. 'I'll groom the horses,' he told Primus. 'They'll catch a chill otherwise.'

The tall man rested his huge hand on Tristran's shoulder. 'Good lad. I'll send a pot-boy out with some burnt ale for you.'

Tristran thought about the star as he brushed down the horses and picked out their hooves. What would he say? What would *she* say? He was brushing the last of the horses when a dull-looking pot-girl came out to him with a tankard of steaming wine.

'Put it down over there,' he told her. 'I'll drink it with goodwill as soon as my hands are free.' She put it down on the top of a tack box, and went out, without saying anything.

It was then that the horse in the end stall got to its feet and began to kick against the door.

'Settle down, there,' called Tristran, 'settle down, fellow, and I'll see if I cannot find warm oats and bran for all of you.'

There was a large stone in the stallion's inside front hoof, and Tristran removed it with care. *Madam*, he had decided he would say, *please accept my heartfelt and most humble apologies. Sir*, the star would say in her turn, *that I shall do with all my heart. Now, let us go to your village, where you shall present me to your true love, as a token of your devotion to her* . . .

His ruminations were interrupted by an enormous clattering, as a huge white horse – but, he realized immediately, it was not a horse – kicked down the door of its stall, and came charging, violently, towards him, its horn lowered.

Tristran threw himself onto the straw on the stable floor, his arms about his head.

Moments passed. He raised his head. The unicorn had stopped in front of the tankard, was lowering its horn into the mulled wine.

Awkwardly, Tristran got to his feet. The wine was steaming and bubbling, and it came to Tristran then – the information surfacing from some long-forgotten fairy tale or piece of children's lore – that a unicorn's horn was proof against . . .

'Poison?' he whispered, and the unicorn raised its head, and stared into Tristran's eyes, and Tristran knew that it was the truth. His heart was pounding hard in his chest. Around the inn the wind was screaming like a witch in her madness.

Tristran ran to the stable door, then he stopped, and thought. He fumbled in his tunic pocket, finding the lump of wax, which was all that remained of his candle, with a dried copper-coloured leaf sticking to it. He peeled the leaf away from the wax with care. Then he raised the leaf to his ear, and listened to what it told him.

***

'Wine, milord?' asked the middle-aged woman in the long red dress, when Primus had entered the inn.

'I am afraid not,' he said. 'I have a personal superstition

that, until the day I see my brother's corpse cold on the ground before me, I shall drink only my own wine, and eat only food I have obtained and prepared myself. This I shall do here, if you have no objection. I shall, of course, pay you as if it were your own wine I was drinking. If I might trouble you to put this bottle of mine near the fire to take the chill from it? Now, I have a companion on my journey, a young man who is attending to the horses; he has sworn no such oath, and I am sure that if you could send him a mug of burnt ale it would help take the chill from his bones . . .?'

The pot-maid bobbed a curtsey, and she scuttled back to the kitchens.

'So, mine host,' said Primus to the white-bearded innkeeper, 'how are your beds here at the back of beyond? Have you straw mattresses? Are there fires in the bedrooms? And I note with increasing pleasure that there is a bathtub in front of your fireplace – if there's a fresh copper of steaming water, I shall have a bath later. But I shall pay you no more than a small silver coin for it, mind.'

The innkeeper looked to his wife, who said, 'Our beds are good, and I shall have the maid make up a fire in the bedroom for you and your companion.'

Primus removed his dripping black robe and hung it by the fire, beside the star's still-damp blue dress. Then he turned, and saw the young lady sitting at the table. 'Another guest?' he said. 'Well-met, milady, in this noxious weather.' At that, there was a loud clattering from the stable next door. 'Something must have disturbed the horses,' said Primus, concerned.

'Perhaps the thunder,' said the innkeeper's wife.

'Aye, perhaps,' said Primus. Something else was occupying his attention. He walked over to the star and stared into her eyes for several heartbeats. 'You . . .' he hesitated. Then, with certainty, 'You have my father's stone. You have the Power of Stormhold.'

The girl glared up at him with eyes the blue of sky. 'Well,

then,' she said. 'Ask me for it, and I can have done with the
stupid thing.'

The innkeeper's wife hurried over, and stood at the head
of the table. 'I'll not have you bothering the other guests now,
my dearie-ducks,' she told him, sternly.

Primus's eyes fell upon the knives upon the wood of the
tabletop. He recognised them: there were tattered scrolls in
the vaults of Stormhold in which those knives were
pictured, and their names were given. They were old things,
from the First Age of the world.

The front door of the inn banged open.

'Primus!' called Tristran, running in. 'They have tried to
poison me!'

The Lord Primus reached for his short-sword, but even as
he went for it the witch-queen took the longest of the knives,
and drew the blade of it, in one smooth, practical movement,
across his throat . . .

For Tristran, it all happened too fast to follow. He entered,
saw the star and Lord Primus, and the innkeeper and his
strange family, and then the blood was spurting in a crimson
fountain in the firelight.

'Get him!' called the woman in the scarlet dress. 'Get the
brat!'

Billy and the maid ran toward Tristran; and it was then
that the unicorn entered the inn.

Tristran threw himself out of the way. The unicorn reared
up on its hind legs, and a blow from one of its sharp hooves
sent the pot-maid flying.

Billy lowered his head and ran, headlong, at the unicorn,
as if he were about to butt it with his forehead. The unicorn
lowered its head also, and Billy the Innkeeper met his
unfortunate end.

'*Stupid!*' screamed the innkeeper's wife, furiously, and she
advanced upon the unicorn, a knife in each hand, blood
staining her right hand and forearm the same colour as her
dress.

Tristran had thrown himself onto his hands and knees, and had crawled toward the fireplace. In his left hand he had hold of the lump of wax, all that remained of the candle that had brought him here. He had been squeezing it in his hand until it was soft and malleable.

'This had better ought to work,' said Tristran to himself. He hoped that the tree had known what she was talking about.

Behind him, the unicorn screamed in pain.

Tristran ripped a lace from his jerkin and closed the wax around it.

'What is happening?' asked the star, who had crawled toward Tristran on her hands and knees.

'I don't really know,' he admitted.

The witch-woman howled, then; the unicorn had speared her with its horn, through the shoulder. It lifted her off the ground, triumphantly, preparing to hurl her to the ground and then to dash her to death beneath its sharp hooves, when, impaled as she was, the witch-woman swung around and thrust the point of the longer of the rock-glass knives into the unicorn's eye and far into its skull.

The beast dropped to the wooden floor of the inn, blood dripping from its side and from its eye and from its open mouth. First it fell to its knees, and then it collapsed, utterly, as the life fled. Its tongue was piebald and it protruded most pathetically from the unicorn's dead mouth.

The witch-queen pulled her body from the horn, and, one hand gripping her wounded shoulder, the other holding her cleaver, she staggered to her feet.

Her eyes scanned the room, alighting on Tristran and the star huddled by the fire. Slowly, agonisingly slowly, she lurched towards them, a cleaver in her hand and a smile upon her face.

'The burning golden heart of a star at peace is so much finer than the flickering heart of a little frightened star,' she told them, her voice oddly calm and detached, coming, as it was, from that blood-bespattered face. 'But even the heart of a star who is afraid and scared is better by far than no heart at all.'

Tristran took the star's hand in his right hand. 'Stand up,' he told her.

'I cannot,' she said, simply.

'Stand, or we die now,' he told her, getting to his feet. The star nodded, and, awkwardly, resting her weight on him, she began to try to pull herself to her feet.

'*Stand, or you die now*?' echoed the witch-queen. 'Oh, you die now, children, standing or sitting. It is all the same to me.' She took another step towards them.

'Now,' said Tristran, one hand gripping the star's arm, the other holding his makeshift candle, 'now, *walk!*'

And he thrust his left hand into the fire.

There was pain, and burning, such that he could have screamed, and the witch-queen stared at him as if he were madness personified.

Then his improvised wick caught, and burned with a steady blue flame, and the world began to shimmer around them. 'Please walk,' he begged the star. 'Don't let go of me.'

And she took an awkward step.

They left the inn behind them, the howls of the witch-queen ringing in their ears.

They were underground, and the candlelight flickered from the wet cave walls; and with their next halting step they were in a desert of white sand, in the moonlight; and with their third step they were high above the earth, looking down on the hills and trees and rivers far below them.

And it was then that the last of the wax ran molten over Tristran's hand, and the burning became impossible for him to bear, and the last of the flame burned out forever.

Chapter Eight

Which Treats of Castles in the Air, and Other Matters

I t was dawn in the mountains. The storms of the last
few days had passed on and the air was clean and cold.
Lord Septimus of Stormhold, tall and crowlike,
walked up the mountain pass, looking about him as he
walked as if he were seeking something he had lost. He was
leading a brown mountain pony, shaggy and small. Where
the pass grew wider he stopped, as if he had found what he
was looking for beside the trail. It was a small, battered
chariot, little more than a goat-cart, which had been tipped
onto its side. Nearby it lay two bodies. The first was that of
a white billy goat, its head stained red with blood. Septimus
prodded the dead goat experimentally with his foot, moving
its head; it had received a deep and fatal wound to its
forehead, equidistant between its horns. Next to the goat was
the body of a young man, his face as dull in death as it must
have been in life. There were no wounds to show how he
had died, nothing but a leaden bruise upon his temple.

Several yards away from these bodies, half-hidden beside
a rock, Septimus came upon the corpse of a man in his
middle years, facedown, dressed in dark clothes. The man's

flesh was pale, and his blood had pooled upon the rocky floor below him. Septimus crouched down beside the body, and, gingerly, lifted its head by the hair; its throat had been cut, expertly, slit from one ear to the other. Septimus stared at the corpse in puzzlement. He *knew* it, yet . . .

And then, in a dry, hacking cough of a noise, he began to laugh. 'Your beard,' he told the corpse, aloud. 'You shaved your beard. As if I would not have known you with your beard gone, Primus.'

Primus, who stood, grey and ghostly, beside his other brothers, said, 'You would have known me, Septimus. But it might have bought me a few moments, wherein I might have seen you before you knew me,' and his dead voice was nothing but the morning breeze rattling the thorn bush.

Septimus stood up. The sun began to rise, then, over the easternmost peak of Mount Belly, framing him in light. 'So I am to be the eighty-second Lord of the Stormhold,' he said to the corpse on the ground, and to himself, 'not to mention the Master of the High Crags, Seneschal of the Spire-Towns, Keeper of the Citadel, Lord High Guardian of Mount Huon and all the rest of it.'

'Not without the Power of Stormhold about your neck you're not, my brother,' said Quintus, tartly.

'And then there's the matter of revenge,' said Secundus, in the voice of the wind howling through the pass. 'You must take revenge upon your brother's killer before anything else, now. It's blood-law.'

As if he had heard them, Septimus shook his head. 'Why could you not have waited just a few more days, brother Primus?' he asked the corpse at his feet. 'I would have killed you myself. I had a fine plan for your death. When I discovered you were no longer on the *Heart of a Dream*, it took me little enough time to steal the ship's boat and get on your trail. And now I must revenge your sad carcass, and all for the honour of our blood and the Stormhold.'

'So Septimus will be the eighty-second Lord of Stormhold,' said Tertius.

'There is a proverbial saying chiefly concerned with warning against too closely calculating the numerical value of unhatched chicks,' pointed out Quintus.

Septimus walked away from the body to piss against a grey boulder. Then he walked back to Primus's corpse. 'If I had killed you, I could leave you here to rot,' he said. 'But because that pleasure was another's, I shall carry you with me a little way, and leave you on a high crag, to be eaten by eagles.' With that, grunting with the effort, he picked up the sticky-fronted body and hauled it over the back of the pony. He fumbled at the corpse's belt, removing the bag of rune stones. 'Thank you for these, my brother,' he said, and he patted the corpse on the back.

'May you choke on them if you do not take revenge on the bitch who slit my gullet,' said Primus, in the voice of the mountain birds waking to greet the new day.

* * *

They sat side by side on a thick, white cumulus cloud the size of a small town. The cloud was soft beneath them, and a little cold. It became colder the deeper into it one sank, and Tristran pushed his burned hand as far as he could down into the fabric of it: it resisted him slightly, but accepted his hand. The interior of the cloud felt spongy and chilly, real and insubstantial at once. The cloud cooled a little of the pain in his hand, allowing him to think more clearly.

'Well,' he said, after some time, 'I'm afraid I've made rather a mess of everything.'

The star sat on the cloud beside him, wearing the robe she had borrowed from the woman in the inn, with her broken leg stretched out on the thick mist in front of her. 'You saved my life,' she said, eventually. 'Didn't you?'

'I suppose I must have done, yes.'

'I hate you,' she said. 'I hated you for everything already, but now I hate you most of all.'

Tristran flexed his burned hand in the blessed cool of the cloud. He felt tired and slightly faint. 'Any particular reason?'

'Because,' she told him, her voice taut, 'now that you have saved my life, you are, by the law of my people, responsible for me, and I for you. Where you go, I must also go.'

'Oh,' he said. 'That's not that bad, is it?'

'I would rather spend my days chained to a vile wolf or a stinking pig or a marsh-goblin,' she told him flatly.

'I'm honestly not that bad,' he told her, 'not when you get to know me. Look, I'm sorry about all that chaining you up business. Perhaps we could start all over again, just pretend it never happened. Here now, my name's Tristran Thorn, pleased to meet you.' He held out his unburned hand to her.

'Mother Moon defend me!' said the star. 'I would sooner take the hand of an—'

'I'm sure you would,' said Tristran, not waiting to find out what he was going to be unflatteringly compared to this time. 'I've *said* I'm sorry,' he told her. 'Let's start afresh. I'm Tristran Thorn. Pleased to meet you.'

She sighed.

The air was thin and chill so high above the ground, but the sun was warm, and the cloud-shapes about them reminded Tristran of a fantastical city or an unearthly town. Far, far below he could see the real world: the sunlight pricking out every tiny tree, turning every winding river into a thin silver snail-trail glistening and looping across the landscape of Faerie.

'Well?' said Tristran.

'Aye,' said the star. 'It is a mighty joke, is it not? Whither thou goest, there I must go. Even if it kills me.' She swirled the surface of the cloud with her hand, rippling the mist. Then, momentarily, she touched her hand to Tristran's. 'My sisters called me Yvaine,' she told him. 'For I was an evening star.'

'Look at us,' he said. 'A fine pair. You with your broken leg, me with my hand.'

'Show me your hand.'

He pulled it from the cool of the cloud: his hand was red, and blisters were coming up on each side of it and on the back of it, where the flames had licked against his flesh.

'Does it hurt?' she asked.

'Yes,' he said. 'Quite a lot, really.'

'Good,' said Yvaine.

'If my hand had not been burned, you would probably be dead now,' he pointed out. She had the grace to look down, ashamed. 'You know,' he added, changing the subject, 'I left my bag in that madwoman's inn. We have nothing now, save the clothes we stand up in.'

'Sit down in,' corrected the star.

'There's no food, no water, we're half a mile or so above the world with no way of getting down, and no control over where the cloud is going. And both of us are injured. Did I leave anything out?'

'You forgot the bit about clouds dissipating and vanishing into nothing,' said Yvaine. 'They do that. I've seen them. I could not survive another fall.'

Tristran shrugged. 'Well,' he said. 'We're probably doomed, then. But we may as well have a look around while we're up here.'

He helped Yvaine to her feet and, awkwardly, the two of them took several faltering steps on the cloud. Then Yvaine sat down again. 'This is no use,' she told him. 'You go and look around. I will wait here for you.'

'Promise?' he asked. 'No running away this time?'

'I swear it. On my mother the moon I swear it,' said Yvaine, sadly. 'You saved my life.'

And with that Tristran had to content himself.

***

Her hair was mostly grey, now, and her face was pouched, and wrinkled at the throat and eyes and at the corners of the mouth. There was no colour to her face, although her skirt was a vivid, bloody splash of scarlet; it had been ripped at the shoulder, and beneath the rip could be seen, puckered and obscene, a deep scar. The wind whipped her hair about her face as she drove the black carriage on through the Barrens. The four stallions stumbled often: thick sweat dripped from their flanks and a bloody foam dripped from their lips. Still, their hooves pounded along the muddy path through the Barrens, where nothing grows.

The witch-queen, oldest of the Lilim, reined in the horses beside a pinnacle of rock the colour of verdigris, which jutted from the marshy soil of the Barrens like a needle. Then, as slowly as might be expected from any lady no longer in her first, or even her second, youth, she climbed down from the driver's seat to the wet earth.

She walked around the coach, and opened the door. The head of the dead unicorn, her dagger still in its cold eye-socket, flopped down as she did so. The witch clambered up into the coach, and pulled open the unicorn's mouth. Rigor mortis was starting to set in, and the jaw opened only with difficulty. The witch-woman bit down, hard, on her own tongue, bit hard enough that the pain was metal-sharp in her mouth, bit down until she could taste the blood. She swirled it around in her mouth, mixing the blood with spittle (she could feel that several of her front teeth were beginning to come loose), then she spat onto the dead unicorn's piebald tongue. Blood flecked her lips and chin. She grunted several syllables that shall not be recorded here, then pushed the unicorn's mouth closed once more. 'Get out of the coach,' she told the dead beast.

Stiffly, awkwardly, the unicorn raised its head. Then it moved its legs, like a newborn foal or fawn just learning to walk, and twitched and pushed itself up onto all fours and, half climbing, half falling, it tumbled out of the carriage door and onto the mud, where it raised itself to its feet. Its left side, upon which it had lain in the coach, was swollen and dark with blood and fluids. Half-blind, the dead unicorn stumbled toward the green rock needle until it reached a depression at its base, where it dropped to the knees of its forelegs in a ghastly parody of prayer.

The witch-queen reached down and pulled her knife from out of the beast's eye-socket. She sliced across its throat. Blood started to ooze, too slowly, from the gash she had made. She walked back to the carriage and returned with her cleaver. Then she began to hack at the unicorn's neck, until she had separated it from the body, and the severed head tumbled into the rock hollow, now filling with a dark red puddle of brackish blood.

She took the unicorn's head by the horn and placed it beside the body, on the rock; thereupon she looked with her hard, grey eyes into the red pool she had made. Two faces stared out at her from the puddle: two women, older by far in appearance than she was now.

'Where is she?' asked the first face, peevishly. 'What have you done with her?'

'Look at you!' said the second of the Lilim. 'You took the last of the youth we had saved – I tore it from the star's breast myself, long, long ago, though she screamed and writhed and carried on ever-so. From the looks of you, you've squandered most of the youth already.'

'I came so close,' said the witch-woman to her sisters in the pool. 'But she had a unicorn to protect her. Now I have the unicorn's head, and I will bring it back with me, for it's long enough since we had fresh ground unicorn's horn in our arts.'

'Unicorn's horn be damned,' said her youngest sister. 'What about the star?'

'I cannot find her. It is almost as if she were no longer in Faerie.'

There was a pause.

'No,' said one of her sisters. 'She is still in Faerie. But she is going to the Market at Wall, and that is too close to the world on the other side of the wall. Once she goes into that world, she will be lost to us.'

For they each of them knew that, were the star to cross the wall and enter the world of things as they are, she would become, in an instant, no more than a pitted lump of metallic rock that had fallen, once, from the heavens: cold and dead and of no more use to them.

'Then I shall go to Diggory's Dyke and wait there, for all who go to Wall must pass that way.'

The reflections of the two old women gazed disapprovingly out of the pool. The witch-queen ran her tongue over her teeth (*that one at the top will be out by nightfall*, she thought, *the way it wobbles so*) and then she spat into the bloody pool. The ripples spread across it, erasing all traces of the Lilim; now the pool reflected only the sky over the Barrens and the faint white clouds far above them.

She kicked the headless corpse of the unicorn so it tumbled over onto its side. Then she took up its head, and she carried it with her up to the driver's seat. She placed it beside her, picked up the reins and whipped the restive horses into a tired trot.

***

Tristran sat at the top of the spire of cloud and wondered why none of the heroes of the penny dreadfuls he used to read so avidly were ever hungry. His stomach rumbled, and his hand hurt him so.

Adventures are all very well in their place, he thought, *but there's a lot to be said for regular meals and freedom from pain*.

Still, he was alive, and the wind was in his hair, and the cloud was scudding through the sky like a galleon at full sail.

Looking out over the world from above, he could never remember feeling so alive as he did at that moment. There was a *skyness* to the sky and a *nowness* to the world that he had never seen or felt or realized before.

He understood that he was, in some way, above his problems, just as he was above the world. The pain in his hand was a long way away. He thought about his actions and his adventures, and about the journey ahead of him, and it seemed to Tristran that the whole business was suddenly very small and very straightforward. He stood up on the cloud spire and called 'Halloo!' several times, as loudly as he could. He even waved his tunic over his head, feeling a little foolish as he did so. Then he clambered down the spire; ten feet from the bottom he missed his footing and fell into the misty softness of the cloud.

'What were you shouting about?' asked Yvaine.

'To let people know we were here,' Tristran told her.

'*What* people?'

'You never know,' he told her. 'Better I should call to people who aren't there than that people who *are* there should miss us because I didn't say anything.'

She said nothing in reply to this.

'I've been thinking,' said Tristran. 'And what I've been thinking is this. After we're done with what I need – got you back to Wall, given you to Victoria Forester – perhaps we could do what *you* need.'

'What *I* need?'

'Well, you want to go back, don't you? Up into the sky. To shine again at night. So we can sort that out.'

She looked up at him and shook her head. 'That doesn't happen,' she explained. 'Stars fall. They don't go back up again.'

'You could be the first,' he told her. 'You have to *believe*. Otherwise it will never happen.'

'It *will* never happen,' she told him. 'No more than your shouting is going to attract anyone up here where there isn't anyone. It doesn't matter if I believe it or not, that's just the way things are. How's your hand?'

He shrugged. 'Hurts,' he said. 'How's your leg?'

'Hurts,' she said. 'But not as badly as it did before.'

'Ahoy!' came a voice from far above them. 'Ahoy down there! Parties in need of assistance?'

Glinting golden in the sunlight was a small ship, its sails billowing, and a ruddy, mustachioed face looked down at them from over the side. 'Was that you, young feller-me-lad, a-leaping and cavorting just now?'

'It was,' said Tristran. 'And I think we are in need of assistance, yes.'

'Right-ho,' said the man. 'Get ready to grab the ladder, then.'

'I'm afraid my friend has a broken leg,' he called, 'and I've hurt my hand. I don't think either of us can climb a ladder.'

'Not a problem. We can pull you up.' And with that the man tumbled a long rope ladder over the side of the ship. Tristran caught at it with his good hand, and he held it steady while Yvaine pulled herself onto it, then he climbed on below her. The face vanished from the side of the ship as Tristran and Yvaine dangled awkwardly on the end of the rope ladder.

The wind caught the sky-ship, causing the ladder to pull up from the cloud, and Tristran and Yvaine to spin, slowly, in the air.

'Now, *haul!*' shouted several voices in unison, and Tristran felt them being hauled up several feet. '*Haul! Haul! Haul!*' Each shout signalled them being pulled higher. The cloud upon which they had been sitting was now no longer below them; instead there was a drop of what Tristran supposed must be a mile or more. He held on tightly to the rope, hooking the elbow of his burned hand about the rope ladder.

Another jerk upwards and Yvaine was level with the top of the ship's railing. Someone lifted her with care and placed her upon the deck. Tristran clambered over the railing himself, and tumbled down onto the oaken deck.

The ruddy-faced man extended a hand. 'Welcome aboard,' he said. 'This is the Free Ship *Perdita*, bound on a lightning-hunting expedition. Captain Johannes Alberic, at your service.' He coughed, deep in his chest. And then, before Tristran could say a word in reply, the captain spied Tristran's left hand, and called 'Meggot! Meggot! Blast you, where are you? Over here! Passengers in need of attention. There lad, Meggot'll see to your hand. We eat at six bells. You shall sit at my table.'

Soon a nervous-looking woman with an explosive mop of carrot-red hair – Meggot – was escorting him belowdecks, and smearing a thick, green ointment onto his hand, which cooled it and eased the pain. And then he was being led into the mess, which was a small dining room next to the kitchen (which he was delighted to discover they referred to as the *galley*, just as in the sea stories he had read).

Tristran did indeed get to eat at the captain's table, although there was in fact no other table in the mess. In addition to the captain and Meggot there were five other members of the crew, a disparate bunch who seemed content to let Captain Alberic do all the talking, which he did, with his ale-pot in one hand, and the other hand alternately concerned with holding his stubby pipe and conveying food into his mouth.

The food was a thick soup of vegetables, beans and barley, and it filled Tristran and contented him. To drink, there was the clearest, coldest water Tristran had ever tasted.

The captain asked them no questions about how they came to find themselves high on a cloud, and they volunteered no answers. Tristran was given a berth with Oddness, the first mate, a quiet gentleman with large wings and a bad stammer, while Yvaine berthed in Meggot's cabin, and Meggot herself moved into a hammock.

Tristran often found himself looking back on his time on the *Perdita*, during the rest of his journey through Faerie, as

one of the happiest periods of his life. The crew let him help
with the sails, and even gave him a turn at the wheel from
time to time. Sometimes the ship would sail above dark
storm clouds, as big as mountains, and the crew would fish
for lightning bolts with a small copper chest. The rain and
the wind would wash the deck of the ship, and he often
would find himself laughing with exhilaration, while the
rain ran down his face, and gripping the rope railing with his
good hand to keep from being tumbled over the side by the
storm.

Meggot, who was a little taller and a little thinner than
Yvaine, had lent her several gowns, which the star wore
with relief, taking pleasure in wearing something new on
different days. Often she would climb out to the figurehead,
despite her broken leg, and sit looking down at the ground
below.

**

'How's your hand?' asked the captain.

'A lot better, thank you,' said Tristran. The skin was shiny
and scarred, and he had little feeling in the fingers, but
Meggot's salve had taken most of the pain, and sped the
healing process immeasurably. He had been sitting on deck,
with his legs dangling over the side, looking out.

'We'll be taking anchor in a week, to take provisions, and
a little cargo,' said the captain. 'Might be best if we were to
let you off down there.'

'Oh. Thank you,' said Tristran.

'You'll be closer to Wall. Still a good ten-week journey,
though. Maybe more. But Meggot says she's nearly got your
friend's leg up to snuff. It'll be able to take her weight again
soon.'

They sat, side by side. The captain puffed on his pipe: his
clothes were covered in a fine layer of ash, and when he was
not smoking his pipe he was chewing at the stem, or

excavating the bowl with a sharp metal instrument, or tamping in new tobacco.

'You know,' said the captain, staring off toward the horizon, 'it wasn't entirely fortune that we found you. Well, it *was* fortune that we found you, but it'd also be true to say that I was keeping half an eye out for you. I, and a few others about the place.'

'Why?' said Tristran. 'And how did you know about me?'

In reply, the captain traced a shape with his finger in the condensation on the polished wood.

'It looks like a castle,' said Tristran.

The captain winked at him. 'Not a word to say too loudly,' he said, 'even up here. Think of it as a fellowship.'

Tristran stared at him. 'Do you know a little hairy man, with a hat and an enormous pack of goods?'

The captain tapped his pipe against the side of the boat. A movement of his hand had already erased the picture of the castle. 'Aye. And he's not the only member of the fellowship with an interest in your return to Wall. Which reminds me, you should tell the young lady that if she fancies trying to pass for other than what she is, she might try to give the impression that she eats something – anything – from time to time.'

'I never mentioned Wall in your presence,' said Tristran. 'When you asked where I was came from, I said "Behind us" and when you asked where we were going, I said, "Ahead of us." '

'That's m'boy,' said the captain. 'Exactly.'

Another week passed, on the fifth day of which Meggot pronounced Yvaine's splint ready to come off. She removed the makeshift bandages and the splint, and Yvaine practised hobbling about the decks from bow to stern, holding onto the rails. Soon she was moving about the ship without difficulty, albeit with a slight limp.

On the sixth day there was a mighty storm, and they caught six fine lightning bolts in their copper box. On the seventh day they made port. Tristran and Yvaine said their good-byes to the captain and the crew of the Free Ship *Perdita*. Meggot gave Tristran a small pot of the green salve, for his hand and for Yvaine to rub onto her leg. The captain gave Tristran a leather shoulder-bag filled with dried meats and fruits and fragments of tobacco, a knife and a tinderbox ('Oh, it's no bother, lad. We're taking on provisions here anyway'), while Meggot made Yvaine a gift of a blue silk gown, sewn with tiny silver stars and moons ('For it looks so much better on you than it ever has on me, my dear').

The ship moored beside a dozen other, similar sky-ships, at the top of a huge tree, large enough to support hundreds of dwellings built into the trunk. It was inhabited by people and dwarfs, by gnomes and sylvans and other, even queerer, folk. There were steps around the trunk, and Tristran and the star descended them slowly. Tristran was relieved to be back on something attached to solid ground, and yet, in some way he could never have put into words, he felt disappointed, as if, when his feet touched the earth once more, he had lost something very fine.

It was three days of walking before the harbour-tree disappeared over the horizon.

They travelled West, toward the sunset, along a wide and dusty road. They slept beside hedgerows. Tristran ate fruit and nuts from bushes and trees and he drank from clear streams. They encountered few other people on the road. When they could, they stopped at small farms, where Tristran would put in an afternoon's work in exchange for food and some straw in the barn to sleep upon. Sometimes they would stop in the towns and villages upon the way, to wash, and eat – or, in the star's case, to feign eating – and to room, whenever they could afford it, at the town's inn.

In the town of Simcock-Under-Hill, Tristran and Yvaine had an encounter with a goblin press-gang that might have ended unhappily, with Tristran spending the rest of his life fighting the goblins' endless wars beneath the earth, had it not been for Yvaine's quick thinking and her sharp tongue. In Berinhed's Forest Tristran outfaced one of the great, tawny eagles, who would have carried them both back to its nest to feed its young and was afraid of nothing at all, save fire.

In a tavern in Fulkeston, Tristran gained great renown by reciting from memory Coleridge's 'Kubla Khan,' the Twenty-Third Psalm, the 'Quality of Mercy' speech from *The Merchant of Venice*, and a poem about a boy who stood on the burning deck where all but he had fled, each of which he had been obliged to commit to memory in his school days. He blessed Mrs Cherry for her efforts in making him memorize verse, until it became apparent that the townsfolk of Fulkeston had decided that he would stay with them forever and become the next bard of the town; Tristran and Yvaine were forced to sneak out of the town at the dead of night, and they only escaped because Yvaine persuaded (by some means, on which Tristran was never entirely clear) the dogs of the town not to bark as they left.

The sun burnt Tristran's face to a nut-brown colour, and faded his clothes to the hues of rust and of dust. Yvaine remained as pale as the moon, and she did not lose her limp, no matter how many leagues they covered.

One evening, camped at the edge of a deep wood, Tristran heard something he had never heard before: a beautiful melody, plangent and strange. It filled his head with visions, and filled his heart with awe and delight. The music made him think of spaces without limits, of huge crystalline spheres which revolved with unutterable slowness through the vasty halls of the air. The melody transported him, took him beyond himself.

After what might have been long hours, and might have been only minutes, it ended, and Tristran sighed. 'That was wonderful,' he said. The star's lips moved, involuntarily, into a smile, and her eyes brightened. 'Thank you,' she said. 'I suppose that I have not felt like singing until now.'

'I have never heard anything like it.'

'Some nights,' she told him, 'my sisters and I would sing together. Sing songs like that one, all about the lady our mother, and the nature of time, and the joys of shining and of loneliness.'

'I'm sorry,' he said.

'Don't be,' she told him. 'At least I am still alive. I was lucky to have fallen in Faerie. And I think I was probably lucky to have met you.'

'Thank you,' said Tristran.

'You are welcome,' said the star. She sighed, then, in her turn, and stared up at the sky through the gaps in the trees.

* * *

Tristran was looking for breakfast. He had found some young puffball mushrooms, and a plum tree covered with purple plums which had ripened and dried almost to prunes, when he spotted the bird in the undergrowth.

He made no attempt to catch it (he had had a severe shock some weeks earlier, when, having narrowly failed to capture a large grey-brown hare for his dinner, it had stopped at the edge of the forest, looked at him with disdain, and said, 'Well, I hope you're proud of yourself, that's all,' and had scampered off into the long grass) but he was fascinated by it. It was a remarkable bird, as large as a pheasant, but with feathers of all colours, garish reds and yellows and vivid blues. It looked like a refugee from the tropics, utterly out of place in this green and ferny wood. The bird started in fear as he approached it, hopping awkwardly as he came closer and letting out cries of sharp distress.

Tristran dropped to one knee next to it, murmuring reassurances. He reached out to the bird. The difficulty was obvious: a silver chain attached to the bird's foot had become entangled in the twisted stub of a jutting root, and the bird was caught there by it, unable to move.

Carefully, Tristran unwound the silver chain, unhooking it

from the root, while stroking the bird's ruffled plumage with his left hand. 'There you go,' he said to the bird. 'Go home.'

But the bird made no move to leave him. Instead it stared into his face, its head cocked on one side. 'Look,' said Tristran, feeling rather odd and self-conscious, 'someone will probably be worried about you.' He reached down to pick up the bird.

Something hit him, then, stunning him; although he had been still, he felt as if he had just run at full tilt into an invisible wall. He staggered, and nearly fell.

'Thief!' shouted a cracked old voice. 'I shall turn your bones to ice and roast you in front of a fire! I shall pluck your eyes out and tie one to a herring and t'other to a seagull, so the twin sights of sea and sky shall take you into madness! I shall make your tongue into a writhing worm and your fingers shall become razors, and fire ants shall itch your skin, so each time you scratch yourself –'

'There is no need to belabour your point,' said Tristran to the old woman. 'I did not steal your bird. Its chain was snagged upon a root, and I had just freed it.'

She glared at him suspiciously from below her mop of iron-grey hair. Then she scurried forward, and picked up the bird. She held it up, and whispered something to it, and it replied with an odd, musical chirp. The old woman's eyes narrowed. 'Well, perhaps what you say is not a complete pack of lies,' she admitted, extremely grudgingly.

'It's not a pack of lies at all,' said Tristran, but the old woman and her bird were already halfway across the glade, so he gathered up his puffballs and his plums, and he walked back to where he had left Yvaine.

She was sitting beside the path, rubbing her feet. Her hip pained her, and so did her leg, while her feet were becoming more and more sensitive. Sometimes at night Tristran would hear her sobbing softly to herself. He hoped the moon would send them another unicorn, and knew that she would not.

'Well,' said Tristran to Yvaine, 'that was odd.' He told her

about the events of the morning, and thought that that was
the end of it.

He was, of course, wrong. Several hours later Tristran and
the star were walking along the forest path when they were
passed by a brightly painted caravan, pulled by two grey
mules and driven by the old woman who had threatened to
change his bones to ice. She reined in her mules and crooked
a bony finger at Tristran. 'Come here, lad,' she said.

He walked over to her warily. 'Yes, ma'am?'

'Seems I owe you an apology,' she said. 'Seems you were
telling the truth. Jumped to a conclusion.'

'Yes,' said Tristran.

'Let me look at you,' she said, climbing down into the
roadway. Her cold finger touched the soft place beneath
Tristran's chin, forcing his head up. His hazel eyes stared
into her old green eyes. 'You look honest enough,' she said.
'You can call me Madame Semele. I'm on my way to Wall, for
the market. I was thinking that I'd welcome a boy to work my
little flower-stall – I sells glass flowers, you know, the
prettiest things that ever you did see. You'd be a fine market-
lad, and we could put a glove over that hand of yours, so
you'd not scare the customers. What d'ye say?'

Tristran pondered, and said, 'Excuse me,' and went over
and conferred with Yvaine. Together they walked back to the
old woman.

'Good afternoon,' said the star. 'We have discussed your
offer, and we thought that –'

'*Well?*' asked Madame Semele, her eyes fixed upon
Tristran. 'Don't just stand there like a dumb thing! Speak!
Speak! Speak!'

'I have no desire to work for you at the market,' said
Tristran, 'for I have business of my own that I shall need to
deal with there. However, if we could ride with you, my
companion and I are willing to pay you for our passage.'

Madame Semele shook her head. 'That's of no use to me. I
can gather my own firewood, and you'd just be another

weight for Faithless and Hopeless to pull. I take no passengers.' She climbed back up into the driver's seat.

'But,' said Tristran, 'I would pay you.'

The harridan cackled with scorn. 'There's never a thing you could possess that I would take for your passage. Now, if you'll not work for me at the market at Wall, then be off with you.'

Tristran reached up to the buttonhole of his jerkin, and felt it there, as cold and perfect as it had been through all his journeyings. He pulled it out, and held it up to the old woman between finger and thumb. 'You sell glass flowers, you say,' he said. 'Would you be interested in this one?'

It was a snowdrop made of green glass and white glass, cunningly fashioned: it seemed as if it had been plucked from the meadow grass that very morning, and the dew was still upon it. The old woman squinted at it for a heartbeat, looking at its green leaves and its tight white petals, then she let out a screech: it might have been the anguished cry of some bereft bird of prey. 'Where did you get that?' she cried. 'Give it to me! Give it to me this instant!'

Tristran closed his finger about the snowdrop, concealing it from view, and he took a couple of steps backwards. 'Hmm,' he said aloud. 'It occurs to me now that I have a deep fondness for this flower, which was a gift from my father when I commenced my travels, and which, I suspect, carries with it a tremendous personal and familial importance. Certainly it has brought me luck, of one kind or another. Perhaps I would be better off keeping the flower, and my companion and I can walk to Wall.'

Madame Semele seemed torn between her desire to threaten and to cajole, and the emotions chased each other so nakedly across her face that she seemed almost to vibrate with the effort of keeping them in check. And then she took herself in hand and said, in a voice that cracked with self-control, 'Now, now. No need to be hasty. I am certain that a deal can be struck between us.'

'Oh,' said Tristran, 'I doubt it. It would need to be a very fine deal, to interest me, and it would need certain guarantees of safe-conduct and such safeguards as to assure that your behaviour and actions toward me and my companion remained at all times benign.'

'Let me see the snowdrop again,' pleaded the old woman.

The bright-coloured bird, its silver chain about one leg, fluttered out of the open door of the caravan, and gazed down at the proceedings beneath.

'The poor thing,' said Yvaine, 'chained up like that. Why do you not set her free?'

But the old woman did not answer her, ignoring her, or so Tristran thought, and said, 'I will transport you to Wall, and I swear upon my honour and upon my true name that I will take no action to harm you upon the journey.'

'Or by inaction, or indirect action, allow harm to come to me or my companion.'

'As you say.'

Tristran thought for a moment. He certainly did not trust the old woman. 'I wish you to swear that we shall arrive in Wall in the same manner and condition and state that we are in now, and that you will give us board and lodging upon the way.'

The old woman clucked, then nodded. She clambered down from the caravan once more, and hawked, then spat into the dust. She pointed to the glob of spittle. 'Now you,' she said. Tristran spat next to it. With her foot she rubbed both wet patches, so they conjoined. 'There,' she said. 'A bargain's a bargain. Give me the flower.'

The greed and hunger were so obvious in her face that Tristran was now certain he could have made a better deal, but he gave the old woman his father's flower. As she took it from him, her face broke into a gap-toothed grin. 'Why, I do think that this is the superior of the one that damnable child gave away almost twenty years gone. Now, tell me, young man,' she asked, looking up at Tristran with her sharp old eyes, 'do you know what manner of thing you have been wearing in your buttonhole?'

'It is a flower. A glass flower.'

The old woman laughed so hard and so suddenly that Tristran thought that she was choking. 'It is a frozen charm,' she said. 'A thing of power. Something like this can perform wonders and miracles in the right hands. Watch.' She held the snowdrop above her head then brought it slowly down, so it brushed Tristran's forehead.

For but a heartbeat he felt most peculiar, as if thick, black treacle were running through his veins in place of blood; then the shape of the world changed. Everything became huge and towering. It seemed as if the old woman herself was now a giantess, and his vision was blurred and confused.

Two huge hands came down and picked him up, gently. ' 'Tain't the biggest of caravans,' said Madame Semele, her voice a low, slow liquid boom. 'And I shall keep to the letter of my oath, for you shall not be harmed, and you shall be boarded and lodged on your journey to Wall.' And then she dropped the dormouse into the pocket of her apron and she clambered onto the caravan.

'And what do you propose to do to me?' asked Yvaine, but she was not entirely surprised when the woman did not reply. She followed the old woman into the dark interior of the caravan. There was but one room; along one wall was a large showcase made of leather and pine, with a hundred pigeonholes in it, and it was in one of these pigeonholes, in a bed of soft thistledown, that the old woman placed the snowdrop. Along the other wall was a small bed, with a window above it, and a large cupboard.

Madame Semele bent down and pulled a wooden cage from the cluttered space beneath her bed, and she took the blinking dormouse from her pocket and placed it into the cage. Then she took a handful of nuts and berries and seeds from a wooden bowl and placed them inside the cage, which she hung from a chain in the middle of the caravan.

'There we go,' she said. 'Board *and* lodging.'

Yvaine had watched all this with curiosity from her seat on the old woman's bed. 'Would I be correct,' she asked politely, 'in concluding from the evidence to hand (to wit, that you have not looked at me, or if you have your eyes have slipped over me, that you have not spoken a word to me, and that you have changed my companion into a small animal with no such provision for myself) that you can neither see me nor hear me?'

The witch made no reply. She walked up to the driver's seat, sat down and took up the reins. The exotic bird hopped up beside her and it chirruped, once, curiously.

'Of course I have kept my word – to the letter,' said the old woman, as if in reply. 'He shall be transformed back at the market meadow, so shall regain his own form before he comes to Wall. And after I have turned him back, I shall make you human again, for I still have to find a better servant than you are, silly slut. I could not have been doing with him underfoot all the livelong day, poking and prying and asking questions, and I'd've had to've fed him into the bargain, more than nuts and seeds.' She hugged herself tightly, and swayed back and forth. 'Oh, you'll have to get up pretty early in the morning to put one past me. And I do believe that that bumpkin's flower was even finer than the one you lost to me, all those years ago.'

She clicked her tongue, and shook the reins, and the mules began to amble down the forest track.

While the witch drove, Yvaine rested upon her musty bed. The caravan clacked and lurched its way through the forest. When it stopped, she would awake, and rise. While the witch slept Yvaine would sit on the roof of the caravan and look up at the stars. Sometimes the witch's bird would sit with her and then she would pet it and make a fuss of it, for it was good to have something about that acknowledged her existence. But when the witch was about, the bird ignored her utterly.

Yvaine also cared for the dormouse, who spent most of his time fast asleep, curled up with his head between his paws. When the witch was off gathering firewood or fetching water, Yvaine would open up his cage, and stroke him, and talk to him, and, on several occasions, she sang to him, although she could not tell whether anything of Tristran remained in the dormouse, who stared up at her with placid, sleepy eyes, like droplets of black ink, and whose fur was softer than down.

Her hip did not pain her, now that she was not walking every day, and her feet did not hurt her so much. She would always limp, she knew, for Tristran was no surgeon when it came to mending a broken bone although he had done the best he could. Meggot had acknowledged as much.

When, as happened infrequently, they encountered other people, the star did her best to stay out of sight. However, she soon learned that, even should someone talk to her within the witch's hearing – should someone, as once a woodcutter did, point to her, and ask Madame Semele about her – the witch never seemed able to perceive Yvaine's presence, or even to hear anything pertaining to her existence.

And so the weeks passed, in a rattling, bone-jarring sort of a way, in the witch's caravan, for the witch, and the bird, and the dormouse, and the fallen star.

Chapter Nine

Which Deals Chiefly With the Events at Diggory's Dyke

❋ ✳

☀

✦

✳

Diggory's Dyke was a deep cut between two chalk Downs – high, green hills, where a thin layer of green grass and reddish earth covered the chalk, and there was scarcely soil enough for trees. The Dyke looked, from a distance, like a white chalk gash on a green velvet board. Local legend had it that the cut was dug, in a day and a night, by one Diggory, using a spade that had once been a sword blade before Wayland Smith had melted it down and beaten it out, on his journey into Faerie from Wall. There were those who said the sword had once been Flamberge, and others, that it was once the sword Balmung; but there were none who claimed to know just who Diggory had been, and it might all have been stuff and nonsense. Anyway, the path to Wall went through Diggory's Dyke, and any foot-traveller or any person going by any manner of wheeled vehicle went through the Dyke, where the chalk rose on either side of you like thick white walls, and the Downs rose up above them like the green pillows of a giant's bed.

In the middle of the Dyke, beside the path, was what appeared at first glance to be little more than a heaped pile of sticks and twigs. A closer inspection would have revealed it to be something in nature partway between a small shed and a large wooden teepee, with a hole in the roof through which grey smoke occasionally could be seen to trickle out.

The man in black had been giving the pile of sticks as close an inspection as he could for two days now, from the top of the Downs far above and, when he dared chance it, from closer. The hut, he had established, was inhabited by a woman of advanced years. She had no companions, and no obvious occupation, apart from that of stopping each and every lone traveller and each conveyance that passed through the Dyke, and passing the time of day.

She seemed harmless enough, but Septimus had not become the only surviving male member of his immediate family by trusting appearances, and this old woman had, he was certain of it, slit Primus's throat.

The obligations of revenge demanded a life for a life; they did not specify any way that the life should be taken. Now, by temperament, Septimus was one of nature's poisoners. Blades and blows and booby traps were well enough in their way, but a vial of clear liquid, any trace of taste or odour gone when it was admixtured with food, that was Septimus's *metier*.

Unfortunately the old woman seemed to take no food she did not gather or trap herself, and while he contemplated leaving a steaming pie at the door to her house, made of ripe apples and lethal baneberries, he dismissed it soon enough as impractical. He pondered rolling a chalk boulder down from the hills above her, dropping it onto her little house; but he could not be certain that he would hit her with it. He wished he was more of a magician – he had some of the locating ability that ran, patchily, in his family line, and a few minor magics he had learned or stolen over the years, but nothing that would be of use to him now, when he needed to invoke floods or hurricanes or lightning strikes. So Septimus observed his victim-to-be as a cat watches a mouse hole, hour after hour, by night and by day.

It was past the mid-hour of the night, and was quite moonless and dark, when Septimus finally crept to the door of the house of sticks, with a firepot in one hand and a book of romantic poetry and a blackbird's nest, into which he had placed several fircones, in the other. Hanging from his belt was a club of oak-wood, its head studded with brass nails. He listened at the door, but could hear nothing but a rhythmic breathing, and, once in a while, a sleeping grunt. His eyes were used to the darkness, and the house stood out against the white chalk of the Dyke. He crept around to the side of the building, where he could keep the door in sight.

First he tore the pages from the book of poems, and crumpled each poem into a ball or a paper twist, which he pushed into the sticks of the shack's wall, at ground level. On top of the poems he placed the fircones. Next, he opened the firepot, and with his knife he fished a handful of waxed linen scraps from the lid, dipped them into the glowing charcoal of the pot and, when they were burning well, he placed them on the paper twists and the cones, and he blew gently on the flickering yellow flames until the pile caught. He dropped dry twigs from the bird's nest onto the little fire, which crackled in the night and began to blossom and grow. The dry sticks of the wall smoked gently, forcing Septimus to suppress a cough, and then they caught fire, and Septimus smiled.

Septimus returned to the door of the hut, hefting his wooden club on high. *For*, he had reasoned, *either the hag will burn with her house, in which case my task is done; or, she will smell the smoke and wake, affrighted and distracted, and she will run from the house, whereupon I shall beat her head with my club, staving it in before she can utter a word. And she will be dead, and I will be revenged.*

'It is a fine plan,' said Tertius in the crackling of the dry wood. 'And once he has killed her, he can go on to obtain the Power of Stormhold.'

'We shall see,' said Primus, and his voice was the wail of a distant night bird.

Flames licked at the little wooden house, and grew and blossomed on its sides with a bright yellow-orange flame. No one came to the door of the hut. Soon, the place was an inferno, and Septimus was forced to take several steps backwards, from the intensity of the heat. He smiled, widely and triumphantly, and he lowered his club.

There came a sharp pain to the heel of his foot. He twisted, and saw a small bright-eyed snake, crimson in the fire's glow, with its fangs sunk deep into the back of his leather boot. He flung his club at it, but the little creature pulled back from his heel, and looped, at great speed, away behind one of the white chalk boulders.

The pain in his heel began to subside. *If there was poison in its bite*, thought Septimus, *the leather will have taken much of it. I shall bind my leg at the calf, and then I shall remove my boot, and make a cross-shaped incision in the place where I was bitten, and I shall suck out the serpent's venom.* So thinking, he sat down upon a chalk boulder in the fire's light, and he tugged at his boot. It would not come off. His foot felt numb, and he realized that the foot must be swelling fast. *Then I shall cut the boot off*, he thought. He raised his foot to the level of his thigh; for a moment he thought his world was going dark, and then he saw that the flames, which had illuminated the Dyke like a bonfire, were gone. He felt chilled to the bone.

'So,' said a voice from behind him, soft as a silken strangling-rope, sweet as a poisoned lozenge, 'you thought that you would warm yourself at the burning of my little cottage. Did you wait at the door to beat out the flames should they prove not to my liking?'

Septimus would have answered her, but his jaw muscles were clenched, his teeth gritted hard together. His heart was pounding inside his chest like a small drum, not in its usual steady march but in a wild, arrhythmic abandon. He could feel every vein and artery in his body threading fire through his frame, if it was not ice that they pumped: he could not tell.

An old woman stepped into his view. She looked like the woman who had inhabited the wooden hut, but older, so much older. Septimus tried to blink, to clear his tearing eyes, but he had forgotten how to blink, and his eyes would not close.

'You should be ashamed of yourself,' said the woman. 'Attempting arson and violence upon the person of a poor old lady living upon her own, who would be entirely at the mercy of every passing vagabond, were it not for the kindness of her little friends.'

And she picked something up from the chalky ground and placed it about her wrist, then she walked back into the hut, which was miraculously unburned, or restored, Septimus did not know which and did not care.

His heart juddered and syncopated inside his chest, and if he could have screamed, he would. It was dawn before the pain ended and, in six voices, his older brothers welcomed Septimus to their ranks.

Septimus looked down, one last time, on the twisted, still-warm form he had once inhabited, and at the expression in its eyes. Then he turned away.

'There are no brothers left to take revenge on her,' he said, in the voice of the morning curlews, 'and it is none of us will ever be Lord of Stormhold. Let us move on.'

And after he had said that, there were not even ghosts in that place.

* * *

The sun was high in the sky that day when Madame Semele's caravan came lumbering through the chalk cut of Diggory's Dyke.

Madame Semele noticed the soot-blackened wooden hovel beside the road and, as she approached closer, the bent old woman in her faded scarlet dress, who waved at her from beside the path. The woman's hair was white as snow, her skin was wrinkled, and one eye was blind.

'Good day, sister. What happened to your house?' asked Madame Semele.

'Young people today. One of them thought it would be good sport to fire the house of a poor old woman who has never harmed a soul. Well, he learned his lesson soon enough.'

'Aye,' said Madame Semele. 'They always learn. And are never grateful to us for the lesson.'

'There's truth for you,' said the woman in the faded scarlet dress. 'Now, tell me, dear. Who rides with you this day?'

'That,' said Madame Semele, haughtily, 'is none of your never-mind, and I shall thank you to keep yourself to yourself.'

'Who rides with you? Tell me truly, or I shall set harpies to tear you limb from limb and hang your remains from a hook deep beneath the world.'

'And who would you be, to threaten me so?'

The old woman stared up at Madame Semele with one good eye and one milky eye. 'I know you, Ditchwater Sal. None of your damned lip. Who travels with you?'

Madame Semele felt the words being torn from her mouth, whether she would say them or no. 'There are the two mules who pull my caravan, myself, a maid-servant I keep in the form of a large bird, and a young man in the form of a dormouse.'

'Anyone else? Anything else?'

'No one and nothing. I swear it upon the Sisterhood.'

The woman at the side of the road pursed her lips. 'Then

get away with you, and get along with you,' she said.

Madame Semele clucked and shook the reins and the mules began to amble on.

In her borrowed bed in the dark interior of the caravan the star slept on, unaware how close she had come to her doom, nor by how slim a margin she had escaped it.

When they were out of sight of the stick-house and the deathly whiteness of Diggory's Dyke, the exotic bird flapped up onto its perch, threw back its head and whooped and crowed and sang, until Madame Semele told it that she would wring its foolish neck if it would not be quiet. And even then, in the quiet darkness inside the caravan, the pretty bird chuckled and twittered and trilled, and, once, it even hooted like a little owl.

***

The sun was already low in the western sky as they approached the town of Wall. The sun shone in their eyes, half blinding them and turning their world to liquid gold. The sky, the trees, the bushes, even the path itself were golden in the light of the setting sun.

Madame Semele reined in her mules in the meadow, where her stall would be. She unhitched the two mules, and led them to the stream, where she hitched them to a tree. They drank deeply and eagerly.

There were other market-folk and visitors setting up their stalls all over the meadow, putting up tents and hanging draperies from trees. There was an air of expectation that touched everyone and everything, like the golden light of the westering sun.

Madame Semele went into the inside of the caravan and unhooked the cage from its chain. She carried it out into the meadow and put it down on a hillock of grass. She opened the cage door, and picked out the sleeping dormouse with bony fingers. 'Out you come,' she said. The dormouse rubbed its liquid black eyes with its forepaws, and blinked at the fading daylight.

The witch reached into her apron and produced a glass daffodil. With it she touched Tristran's head.

Tristran blinked sleepily, and then he yawned. He ran a hand through his unruly brown hair and looked down at the witch with fierce anger in his eyes. 'Why, you evil old crone—' he began.

'Hush your silly mouth,' said Madame Semele, sharply. 'I got you here, safely and soundly, and in the same condition I found you. I gave you board and I gave you lodging – and if neither of them were to your liking or expectation, well, what is it to me? Now, be off with you, before I change you into a wiggling worm and bite off your head, if it is not your tail. Go! Shoo! Shoo!'

Tristran counted to ten, and then, ungraciously, walked away. He stopped a dozen yards away beside a copse, and waited for the star, who limped down the side of the caravan steps, and came over to him.

'Are you all right?' he asked, genuinely concerned, as she approached.

'Yes, thank you,' said the star. 'She did not ill-use me. Indeed, I do not believe that she ever knew that I was there at all. Is that not peculiar?'

Madame Semele had the bird in front of her now. She touched its plumed head with her glass flower, and it flowed and shifted and became a young woman, in appearance not too much older than Tristran himself, with dark, curling hair and furred, catlike ears. She darted a glance at Tristran, and there was something about those violet eyes that Tristran found utterly familiar, although he could not recall where he had seen them before.

'So, that is the bird's true form,' said Yvaine. 'She was a good companion on the road.' And then the star realized that the silver chain that had kept the bird a captive was still there, now that the bird had become a woman, for it glinted upon her wrist and ankle, and Yvaine pointed this out to Tristran.

'Yes,' said Tristran. 'I can see. It *is* awful. But I'm not sure there's much that we can do about it.'

They walked together through the meadow, toward the gap in the wall. 'We shall visit my parents first,' said Tristran. 'For I have no doubt that they have missed me as I have missed them' – although, truth to tell, Tristran had scarcely given his parents a second thought on his journeyings – 'and then we shall pay a visit to Victoria Forester, and—' It was with this *and* that Tristran closed his mouth. For he could no longer reconcile his old idea of giving the star to Victoria Forester with his current notion that the star was not a thing to be passed from hand to hand, but a true person in all respects and no kind of a thing at all. And yet, Victoria Forester *was* the woman he loved.

Well and all, he would burn that bridge when he came to it, he decided, and for now he would take Yvaine into the village, and deal with events as they came. He felt his spirits lift, and his time as a dormouse had already become nothing more in his head than the remnants of a dream, as if he had merely taken an afternoon nap in front of the kitchen fire and was now wide awake once more. He could almost taste in his mouth the memory of Mr Bromios's best ale, although he realized, with a guilty start, he had forgotten the colour of Victoria Forester's eyes.

The sun was huge and red behind the rooftops of Wall when Tristran and Yvaine crossed the meadow and looked down on the gap in the wall. The star hesitated.

'Do you really want this?' she asked Tristran. 'For I have misgivings.'

'Don't be nervous,' he said. 'Although it's not surprising that you have nerves; my stomach feels as if I had swallowed a hundred butterflies. You shall feel so much better when you are sitting in my mother's parlour, drinking her tea – well, not drinking tea, but there will be tea for you to sip –

why, I swear that for such a guest, and to welcome her boy back home, my mother would break out the best china,' and his hand sought hers and gave it a reassuring squeeze.

She looked at him, and she smiled, gently and ruefully. 'Whither thou goest . . .' she whispered.

Hand in hand the young man and the fallen star approached the gap in the wall.

Chapter Ten

Stardust

It has occasionally been remarked upon that it is as easy to overlook something large and obvious as it is to overlook something small and niggling, and that the large things one overlooks can often cause problems.

Tristran Thorn approached the gap in the wall, from the Faerie side, for the second time since his conception eighteen years before, with the star limping beside him. His head was in a whirl from the scents and the sounds of his native village, and his heart rose within him. He nodded politely to the guards on the gap as he approached, recognizing them both. The young man shifting idly from foot to foot, sipping a pint of what Tristran supposed to be Mr Bromios's best ale, was Wystan Pippin, who had once been Tristran's schoolfellow, although never his friend; while the older man, sucking irritably upon a pipe, which appeared to have gone out, was none other than Tristran's former employer at Monday and Brown's, Jerome Ambrose Brown, Esquire. The men had their backs to Tristran and Yvaine, and were resolutely facing the village as if they thought it sinful to observe the preparations occurring in the meadow behind them.

'Good evening,' said Tristran, politely, 'Wystan. Mister Brown.'

The two men started. Wystan spilled his beer down the front of his jacket. Mr Brown raised his staff and pointed the end of it at Tristran's chest, nervously. Wystan Pippin put down his ale, picked up his staff, and blocked the gap with it.

'Stay where you are!' said Mr Brown, gesturing with the staff, as if Tristran were a wild beast that might spring at him at any moment.

Tristran laughed. 'Do you not know me?' he asked. 'It is me, Tristran Thorn.'

But Mr Brown, who was, Tristran knew, the senior of the guards, did not lower his staff. He looked Tristran up and down, from his worn brown boots to his mop of shaggy hair. Then he stared into Tristran's sun-browned face, and sniffed, unimpressed. 'Even if you are that good-for-nothing Thorn,' he said, 'I see no reason to let either of you people through. We guard the wall, after all.'

Tristran blinked. 'I, too, have guarded the wall,' he pointed out. 'And there are no rules about not letting people through from this direction. Only from the village.'

Mr Brown nodded, slowly. Then he said, as one talks to an idiot, 'And if you are Tristran Thorn – which I'm only conceding for the sake of argument here, for you look nothing like him, and you talk little enough like him either – in all the years you lived here, how many people came through the wall from the meadow side?'

'Why, none that ever I knew of,' said Tristran.

Mr Brown smiled the same smile he had been used to use when he docked Tristran a morning's wages for five minutes' lateness. 'Exactly,' he said. 'There was no rule against it because it doesn't happen. No one comes through from the other side. Not while *I'm* on duty, any road. Now, be off with you, before I take my stick to your head.'

Tristran was dumbfounded. 'If you think I have gone

through, well, everything I've gone through, only to be turned away at the last by a self-important, penny-pinching grocer and by someone who used to crib from me in History . . .' he began, but Yvaine touched his arm and said, 'Tristran, let it go for now. You shall not fight with your own people.'

Tristran said nothing. Then he turned, without a word, and together they walked back up the slope of the meadow. Around them a hodgepodge of creatures and people erected their stalls, hung their flags and wheeled their barrows. And it came to Tristran then, in a wave of something that resembled homesickness, but a homesickness comprised in equal parts of longing and despair, that these might as well be his own people, for he felt he had more in common with them than with the pallid folk of Wall in their worsted jackets and their hobnailed boots.

They stopped and watched a small woman, almost as broad as she was high, do her best to put up her stall. Unasked, Tristran walked over and began to help her, carrying the heavy boxes from her cart to the stall, climbing a tall stepladder to hang an assortment of streamers from a tree branch, unpacking heavy glass carafes and jugs (each one stoppered with a huge, blackened cork and sealed with silvery wax, and filled with a slowly swirling coloured smoke), and placing them on the shelves. As he and the market-woman worked, Yvaine sat on a nearby tree stump and she sang to them in her soft, clean voice the songs of the high stars, and the commoner songs she had heard and learnt from the folk they had encountered on their journeyings.

By the time Tristran and the little woman were done, and the stall was set out for the morrow, they were working by lamplight. The woman insisted on feeding them; Yvaine barely managed to convince her that she was not hungry, but Tristran ate everything he was offered with enthusiasm and, unusually for him, he drank the greater part of a carafe of sweet canary wine, insisting that it tasted no stronger than freshly squeezed grape juice and that it had no effect upon him of any kind. Even so, when the stout little woman offered them the clearing behind her cart to sleep in, Tristran was sleeping drunkenly in moments.

It was a clear, cold night. The star sat beside the sleeping man, who had once been her captor and had become her companion on the road, and she wondered where her hatred had gone. She was not sleepy.

There was a rustle in the grass behind her. A dark-haired woman stood next to her, and together they stared down at Tristran.

'There is something of the dormouse in him still,' said the dark-haired woman. Her ears were pointed and catlike, and she looked little older than Tristran himself. 'Sometimes I wonder if she transforms people into animals, or whether she finds the beast inside us, and frees it. Perhaps there is something about me that is, by nature, a brightly coloured bird. It is something to which I have given much thought, but about which I have come to no conclusions.'

Tristran muttered something unintelligible, and stirred in his sleep. Then he began, gently, to snore.

The woman walked around Tristran, and sat down beside him. 'He seems good-hearted,' she said.

'Yes,' admitted the star. 'I suppose that he is.'

'I should warn you,' said the woman, 'that if you leave these lands for . . . over there . . .' and she gestured toward the village of Wall with one slim arm, from the wrist of which a silver chain glittered, '. . . then you will be, as I understand it, transformed into what you would be in that world: a cold, dead thing, sky-fallen.'

The star shivered, but she said nothing. Instead, she reached across Tristran's sleeping form to touch the silver chain which circled the woman's wrist and ankle and led off into the bushes and beyond.

'You become used to it, in time,' said the woman.

'Do you? Really?'

Violet eyes stared into blue eyes, and then looked away. 'No.'

The star let go of the chain. 'He once caught me with a chain much like yours. Then he freed me, and I ran from him. But he found me and bound me with an obligation, which binds my kind more securely than any chain ever could.'

An April breeze ran across the meadow, stirring the bushes and the trees in one long chilly sigh. The cat-eared woman tossed her curly hair back from her face, and said, 'You are under a prior obligation, are you not? You have something that does not belong to you, which you must deliver to its rightful owner.'

The star's lips tightened. 'Who are you?' she asked.

'I told you. I was the bird in the caravan,' said the woman. 'I know what you are, and I know why the witch-woman never knew that you were there. I know who seeks you and why she needs you. Also, I know the provenance of the topaz stone you wear upon a silver chain about your waist. Knowing this, and what manner of thing you are, I know the obligation you must be under.' She leaned down, and, with delicate fingers, she tenderly pushed the hair from Tristran's face. The sleeping youth neither stirred nor responded.

'I do not think that I believe you, or trust you,' said the star. A night bird cried in a tree above them. It sounded very lonely in the darkness.

'I saw the topaz about your waist when I was a bird,' said the woman, standing up once more. 'I watched, when you bathed in the river, and recognized it for what it was.'

'How?' asked the star. 'How did you recognize it?'

But the dark-haired woman only shook her head and walked back the way that she had come, sparing but one last glance for the sleeping youth upon the grass. And then she was taken by the night.

Tristran's hair had, obstinately, fallen across his face once more. The star leaned down and gently pushed it to one side,

letting her fingers dwell upon his cheek as she did so. He
slept on.

                              ***

Tristran was woken a little after sunrise by a large badger
walking upon its hind legs and wearing a threadbare
heliotrope silk dressing-gown, who snuffled into his ear
until Tristran sleepily opened his eyes, and then said, self-
importantly, 'Party name of Thorn? Tristran of that set?'

'Mm?' said Tristran. There was a foul taste in his mouth,
which felt dry and furred. He could have slept for another
several hours.

'They've been asking about you,' said the badger. 'Down
by the gap. Seems there's a young lady wants to have a word
with you.'

Tristran sat up and grinned widely. He touched the
sleeping star on her shoulder. She opened her sleepy blue
eyes and said, 'What?'

'Good news,' he told her. 'Do you remember Victoria
Forester? I might have mentioned her name once or twice on
our travels.'

'Yes,' she said. 'You might have.'

'Well,' he said, 'I'm off to see her. She's down by the gap.'
He paused. 'Look. Well. Probably best if you stay here. I
wouldn't want to confuse her or anything.'

The star rolled over and covered her head with her arm,
and said nothing else. Tristran decided that she must have
gone back to sleep. He pulled on his boots, washed his face
and rinsed out his mouth in the meadow stream, and then
ran pell-mell through the meadow, toward the village.

The guards on the wall this morning were the Reverend
Myles, the Vicar of Wall, and Mr Bromios, the innkeeper.
Standing between them was a young lady with her back to
the meadow. '*Victoria*!' called Tristran in delight; but then
the young lady turned, and he saw that it was *not* Victoria

Forester (who, he remembered suddenly, and with delight in the knowing, had *grey* eyes. That was what they were: grey. How could he ever have allowed himself to forget?). But who this young lady could have been in her fine bonnet and shawl, Tristran could not say; although her eyes flooded with tears at the sight of him.

'Tristran!' she said. 'It *is* you! They said it was! Oh Tristran! How *could* you? Oh, how could you?' and he realized who the young lady reproaching him must be.

'Louisa?' he said to his sister. And then, 'You have certainly grown while I was away, from a chit of a girl into a fine young lady.'

She sniffed, and blew her nose into a lace-edged linen handkerchief, which she pulled from her sleeve. 'And you,' she told him, dabbing at her cheeks with the handkerchief, 'have turned into a mop-haired raggle-taggle gypsy on your journeyings. But I suppose you look well, and that is a good thing. Come on, now,' and she motioned, impatiently, for him to walk through the gap in the wall, and come to her.

'But the wall –' he said, eyeing the innkeeper and the Vicar a little nervously.

'Oh, as to that, when Wystan and Mister Brown finished their shift last night they repaired to the saloon bar at the *Seventh Pie*, where Wystan happened to mention their meeting with a ragamuffin who claimed to be you, and how they blocked his way. Your way. When news of this reached Father's ears, he marched right up to the *Pie* and gave the both of them such a tongue-lashing and a telling-of-what-for that I could scarcely believe it was him.'

'Some of us were for letting you come back this morning,' said the Vicar, 'and some were for keeping you there until midday.'

'But none of the ones who were for making you wait are on wall duty this morning,' said Mr Bromios. 'Which took a certain amount of jiggery-pokery to organize – and on a day when I should have been seeing to the refreshment stand, I

could point out. Still, it's good to see you back. Come on
through.' And with that he stuck out his hand, and Tristran
shook it with enthusiasm. Then Tristran shook the Vicar's
hand.

'Tristran,' said the Vicar, 'I suppose that you must have
seen many strange sights upon your travels.'

Tristran reflected for a moment. 'I suppose I must have,' he
said.

'You must come to the Vicarage, then, next week,' said the
Vicar. 'We shall have tea, and you must tell me all about it.
Once you're settled back in. Eh?' And Tristran, who had
always held the Vicar in some awe, could do nothing but
nod.

Louisa sighed, a little theatrically, and began to walk,
briskly, in the direction of the *Seventh Magpie*. Tristran ran
along the cobbles to catch her up, and then he was walking
beside her.

'It does my heart good to see you again, my sister,' he said.

'As if we were not all worried sick about you,' she said,
crossly, 'what with all your gallivantings. And you did not
even wake me to say good-bye. Father has been quite
distracted with concern for you, and at Christmas, when you
were not there, after we had eaten the goose and the
pudding, Father took out the port and he toasted absent
friends, and Mother sobbed like a babe, so of course I cried
too, and then Father began to blow his nose into his best
handkerchief and Grandmother and Grandfather Hempstock
insisted upon pulling the Christmas crackers and reading the
jolly mottoes and somehow that only made matters worse,
and, to put it bluntly, Tristran, you quite spoiled our
Christmas.'

'Sorry,' said Tristran. 'What are we doing now? Where are
we going?'

'We are going into the *Seventh Pie*,' said Louisa. 'I should
have thought that was obvious. Mister Bromios said that you
could use his sitting room. There's somebody there who

needs to talk to you.' And she said nothing more as they went into the pub. There were a number of faces Tristran recognized, and the people nodded at him, or smiled, or did not smile, as he walked through the crowds and made his way up the narrow stairs behind the bar to the landing with Louisa by his side. The wooden boards creaked beneath their feet.

Louisa glared at Tristran. And then her lip trembled, and, to Tristran's surprise, she threw her arms about him and hugged him so tightly that he could not breathe. Then, with not another word, she fled back down the wooden stairs.

He knocked at the door to the sitting room, and went in. The room was decorated with a number of unusual objects, of small items of antique statuary and clay pots. Upon the wall hung a stick, wound about with ivy leaves, or rather, with a dark metal cunningly beaten to resemble ivy. Apart from the decorations the room could have been the sitting room of any busy bachelor with little time for sitting. It was furnished with a small chaise longue, a low table upon which was a well-thumbed leather-bound copy of the sermons of Laurence Sterne, a pianoforte, and several leather armchairs, and it was in one of these armchairs that Victoria Forester was sitting.

Tristran walked over to her slowly and steadily, and then he went down upon one knee in front of her, as once he had gone down on his knees before her in the mud of a country lane.

'Oh, please don't,' said Victoria Forester, uncomfortably. 'Please get up. Why don't you sit down over there. In that chair? Yes. That's better.' The morning light shone through the high lace curtains and caught her chestnut hair from behind, framing her face in gold. 'Look at you,' she said. 'You became a man. And your hand. What happened to your hand?'

'I burnt it,' he said. 'In a fire.'

She said nothing in response, at first. She just looked at

him. Then she sat back in the armchair, and looked ahead of
her, at the stick on the wall, or one of Mr Bromios's quaint
old statues perhaps, and she said, 'There are a number of
things I must tell you, Tristran, and none of them will be
easy. I would appreciate it if you said nothing until I have
had a chance to say my piece. So: firstly, and perhaps most
importantly, I must apologize to you. It was my foolishness,
my idiocy, that sent you off on your journeyings. I thought
you were joking . . . no, not joking. I thought that you were
too much the coward, too much of a boy, ever to follow up
on any of your fine, silly words. It was only when you had
gone, and the days passed, and you did not return, that I
realized that you had been in earnest, and by then it was
much too late.

'I have had to live . . . each day . . . with the possibility that
I had sent you to your death.'

She stared ahead of herself as she spoke, and Tristran had
the feeling, which became a certainty, that she had
conducted this conversation in her head a hundred times in
his absence. It was why he could not be permitted to say
anything; this was hard enough on Victoria Forester, and she
would not be able to manage it if he caused her to depart
from her script.

'And I did not play you fair, my poor shop-boy . . . but you
are no longer a shop-boy, are you? . . . since I thought that
your quest was just foolishness, in every way . . .' She
paused, and her hands gripped the wooden arms of the chair,
grasping them so tightly her knuckles first reddened, then
went white. 'Ask me why I would not kiss you that night,
Tristran Thorn.'

'It was your right not to kiss me,' said Tristran. 'I did not
come here to make you sad, Vicky. I did not find you your
star to make you miserable.'

Her head tipped to one side. 'So you *did* find the star we
saw that night?'

'Oh yes,' said Tristran. 'The star is back in the meadow,

though, right now. But I did what you asked me to do.'

'Then do something else for me now. Ask me why I would not kiss you that night. I had kissed you before, when we were younger, after all.'

'Very well, Vicky. Why would you not kiss me, that night?'

'Because,' she said, and there was relief in her voice as she said it, enormous relief, as if it were escaping from her, 'the day before we saw the shooting star, Robert had asked me to marry him. That evening, when I saw you, I had gone to the shop hoping to see him, and to talk to him, and to tell him that I accepted, and he should ask my father for my hand.'

'Robert?' asked Tristran, his head all in a whirl.

'Robert Monday. You worked in his shop.'

'Mister Monday?' echoed Tristran. 'You and Mister Monday?'

'Exactly.' She was looking at him now. 'And then you had to take me seriously and run off to bring me back a star, and not a day would go by when I did not feel as if I had done something foolish and bad. For I promised you my hand, if you returned with the star. And there were some days, Tristran, when I honestly do not know which I thought worse, that you would be killed in the Lands Beyond, all for the love of me, or that you would succeed in your madness, and return with the star, to claim me as your bride. Now, of course, some folks hereabouts told me not to take on so, and that it was inevitable that you would have gone off to the Lands Beyond, of course, it being your nature, and you being from there in the first place, but, somehow, in my heart, I knew I was at fault, and that, one day, you would return to claim me.'

'And you love Mister Monday?' said Tristran, seizing on the only thing in all this he was certain he had understood.

She nodded, and raised her head, so her pretty chin pointed toward Tristran. 'But I gave you my word, Tristran. And I *will* keep my word, and I have told Robert this. I am responsible for all that you have gone through – even for your poor burned hand. And if you want me, then I am yours.'

'To be honest,' he said, 'I think that I am responsible for all that I have done, not you. And it is hard to regret a moment of it, although I missed soft beds from time to time, and I shall never be able to look at another dormouse in quite the same way ever again. But you did not promise me your hand if I came back with the star, Vicky.'

'I didn't?'

'No. You promised me anything I desired.'

Victoria Forester sat bolt upright then, and looked down at the floor. A red spot burned in each pale cheek, as if she had been slapped. 'Do I understand you to be –' she began, but Tristran interrupted her. 'No,' he said. 'I don't think you do, actually. You said you would give me whatever I desire.'

'Yes.'

'Then . . .' He paused. 'Then I desire that you should marry Mister Monday. I desire that you should be married as soon as possible – why, within this very week, if such a thing can be arranged. And I desire that you should be as happy together as ever a man and woman have ever been.'

She exhaled in one low shuddering breath of release. Then she looked at him. 'Do you mean it?' she asked.

'Marry him with my blessing, and we'll be quits and done,' said Tristran. 'And the star will probably think so, too.'

There was a knock at the door. 'Is all well in there?' called a man's voice.

'Everything is very well,' said Victoria. 'Please come in, Robert. You remember Tristran Thorn, do you not?'

'Good morning, Mister Monday,' said Tristran, and he shook Mr Monday's hand, which was sweaty and damp. 'I understand that you are to be married soon. Permit me to tender my congratulations.'

Mr Monday grinned, though it made him look as if he had a toothache. Then he held out a hand for Victoria, and she rose from the chair.

'If you wish to see the star, Miss Forester . . .' said Tristran, but Victoria shook her head.

'I am delighted that you came home safely, Thorn. I trust that I shall see you at our wedding?'

'I'm sure that nothing could give me greater pleasure than to be there,' said Tristran, although he was sure of no such thing.

***

On a normal day it would have been unheard-of for the *Seventh Magpie* to have been so crowded before breakfast, but this was market day, and the Wall-folk and the strangers were crowded into the bar, eating heaped plates of lamb-chops and bacon and mushrooms and fried eggs and black pudding.

Dunstan Thorn was waiting for Tristran in the bar. He stood up when he saw him, walked over and clasped him on the shoulder, without speaking. 'So you made it back without hurt,' he said, and there was pride in his voice.

Tristran wondered if he had grown while he was away; he remembered his father as a bigger man. 'Hello, Father,' he said. 'I hurt my hand a bit.'

'Your mother has breakfast waiting for you, back at the farm,' said Dunstan.

'Breakfast would be wonderful,' admitted Tristran. 'And seeing Mother again, of course. Also we need to talk.' For his mind was still on something that Victoria Forester had said.

'You look taller,' said his father. 'And you are badly in need of a trip to the barber's.' He drained his tankard, and together they left the *Seventh Magpie* and walked out into the morning.

The two Thorns climbed over a stile into one of Dunstan's fields, and, as they walked through the meadow in which he had played as a boy, Tristran raised the matter that had been vexing him, which was the question of his birth. His father

answered him as honestly as he was able to during the long
walk back to the farmhouse, telling his tale as if he were
recounting a story that had happened a very long time ago,
to someone else. A love story.

And then they were at Tristran's old home, where his
sister waited for him, and there was a steaming breakfast on
the stove and on the table, prepared for him, lovingly, by the
woman he had always believed to be his mother.

* * *

Madame Semele adjusted the last of the crystal flowers on
the stall, and eyed the market with disfavour. It was a little
past noon, and the customers had just started to wander
through. None of them had yet stopped at her stall.

'Fewer of them and fewer of them, every nine-year,' she
said. 'Mark my words, soon enough this market will be just
a memory. There's other markets, and other marketplaces, I
am thinking. This market's time is almost over. Another
forty, fifty, sixty years at the most, and it will be done for
good.'

'Perhaps,' said her violet-eyed servant, 'but it does not
matter to me. This is the last of these markets I shall ever
attend.'

Madame Semele glared at her. 'I thought I had long since
beaten all of your insolence out of you.'

'It is not insolence,' said her slave. 'Look.' She held up the
silver chain which bound her. It glinted in the sunlight, but
still, it was *thinner*, more translucent than ever it had been
before; in places it seemed as if it were made not of silver but
of smoke.

'What have you done?' Spittle flecked the old woman's
lips.

'I have done nothing; nothing that I did not do eighteen
years ago. I was bound to you to be your slave until the day
that the moon lost her daughter, if it occurred in a week

when two Mondays came together. And my time with you is almost done.'

***

It was after three in the afternoon. The star sat upon the meadow grass beside Mr Bromios's wine-and-ale-and-food stall, and stared across at the gap in the wall and the village beyond it. Upon occasion, the patrons of the stall would offer her wine or ale or great, greasy sausages, and always she would decline.

'Are you waiting for someone, my dear?' asked a pleasant-featured young woman, as the afternoon dragged on.

'I do not know,' said the star. 'Perhaps.'

'A young man, if I do not mistake my guess, a lovely thing like you.'

The star nodded. 'In a way,' she said.

'I'm Victoria,' said the young woman. 'Victoria Forester.'

'I am called Yvaine,' said the star. She looked Victoria Forester up and down and up again. 'So,' she said, 'you are Victoria Forester. Your fame precedes you.'

'The wedding, you mean?' said Victoria, and her eyes shone with pride and delight.

'A wedding, is it?' asked Yvaine. One hand crept to her waist, and felt the topaz, upon its silver chain. Then she stared at the gap in the wall, and bit her lip.

'Oh you poor thing! What a beast he must be, to keep you waiting so!' said Victoria Forester. 'Why do you not go through, and look for him?'

'Because . . .' said the star, and then she stopped. 'Aye,' she said. 'Perhaps I shall.' The sky above them was striped with grey and white bands of cloud, through which patches of blue could be seen. 'I wish my mother were out,' said the star. 'I would say good-bye to her, first.' And, awkwardly, she got to her feet.

But Victoria was not willing to let her new friend go that

easily, and she was prattling on about banns, and marriage
licenses, and special licenses which could only be issued by
Archbishops, and how lucky she was that Robert knew the
Archbishop. The wedding, it seemed, was set for six days'
time, at midday.

Then Victoria called over a respectable gentleman, greying
at the temples, who was smoking a black cheroot and who
grinned as if he had the toothache. 'And this is Robert,' she
said. 'Robert, this is Yvaine. She's waiting for her young man.
Yvaine, this is Robert Monday. And on Friday next, at midday,
I shall be Victoria Monday. Perhaps you could make something of that, my dear, in your speech at the wedding breakfast
– that on Friday there will be two Mondays together!'

And Mr Monday puffed on his cheroot, and told his bride-
to-be that he would certainly consider it.

'Then,' asked Yvaine, picking her words with care, 'you
are *not* marrying Tristran Thorn?'

'No,' said Victoria.

'Oh,' said the star. 'Good.' And she sat down again.

***

She was still sitting there when Tristran came back through
the gap in the wall, several hours later. He looked distracted,
but brightened up when he saw her. 'Hello, you,' he said,
helping her to her feet. 'Have a good time waiting for me?'

'Not particularly,' she said.

'I'm sorry,' said Tristran. 'I suppose I should have taken
you with me, into the village.'

'No,' said the star, 'You shouldn't have. I live as long as I
am in Faerie. Were I to travel to your world, I would be
nothing but a cold iron stone fallen from the heavens, pitted
and pocked.'

'But I almost took you through with me!' said Tristran,
aghast. 'I tried to, last night.'

'Yes,' she said. 'Which only goes to prove that you are

indeed a ninny, a lackwit, and a . . . a clodpoll.'

'Dunderhead,' offered Tristran. 'You always used to like calling me a dunderhead. And an oaf.'

'Well,' she said, 'you are all those things, and more besides. Why did you keep me waiting like that? I thought something terrible had happened to you.'

'I'm sorry,' he told her. 'I won't leave you again.'

'No,' she said, seriously and with certainty, 'you will not.'

His hand found hers, then. They walked, hand in hand, through the market. A wind began to come up, flapping and gusting at the canvas of the tents and the flags, and a cold rain spat down on them. They took refuge under the awning of a book stall, along with a number of other people and creatures. The stallholder hauled a boxful of books further under the canvas, to ensure that it did not get wet.

'Mackerel sky, mackerel sky, not long wet nor not long dry,' said a man in a black silk top hat to Tristran and Yvaine. He was purchasing a small book bound in red leather from the bookseller.

Tristran smiled and nodded, and, as it became apparent that the rain was easing up, he and Yvaine walked on.

'Which is all the thanks I shall ever get from them, I'll wager,' said the tall man in the top hat to the bookseller, who had not the slightest idea what he was speaking about, and did not care.

'I have said my good-byes to my family,' said Tristran to the star, as they walked. 'To my father, and my mother – my father's wife, perhaps I should say – and to my sister, Louisa. I don't think I shall be going back again. Now we just need to solve the problem of how to put you back up again in the sky. Perhaps I shall come with you.'

'You would not like it, up in the sky,' the star assured him.

'So . . . I take it you will not be marrying Victoria Forester.'

Tristran nodded. 'No,' he said.

'I met her,' said the star. 'Did you know that she is with child?'

'What?' asked Tristran, shocked and surprised.

'I doubt that she knows. She is one, perhaps two moons along.'

'Good lord. How do you know?'

It was the star's turn to shrug. 'You know,' she said, 'I was happy to discover that you are not marrying Victoria Forester.'

'So was I,' he confessed.

The rain began once more, but they made no move to get under cover. He squeezed her hand in his. 'You know,' she said, 'a star and a mortal man . . .'

'Only half mortal, actually,' said Tristran, helpfully. 'Everything I ever thought about myself – who I was, what I am – was a lie. Or sort of. You have no idea how astonishingly liberating that feels.'

'Whatever you are,' she said, 'I just wanted to point out that we can probably never have children. That's all.'

Tristran looked at the star, then, and he began to smile, and he said nothing at all. His hands were on her upper arms. He was standing in front of her, and looking down at her.

'Just so you know, that's all,' said the star, and she leaned forward.

They kissed for the first time then in the cold spring rain, though neither one of them now knew that it was raining. Tristran's heart pounded in his chest as if it were not big enough to contain all the joy that it held. He opened his eyes as he kissed the star. Her sky-blue eyes stared back into his, and in her eyes he could see no parting from her.

***

The silver chain was now nothing but smoke and vapour. For a heartbeat it hung on the air, then a sharp gust of wind and rain blew it out into nothing at all.

'There,' said the woman with the dark, curling hair,

stretching like a cat, and smiling. 'The terms of my servitude are fulfilled, and now you and I are done with each other.'

The old woman looked at her helplessly. 'But what shall I do? I am old. I cannot manage this stall by myself. You are an evil, foolish slattern, so to desert me like this.'

'Your problems are of no concern to me,' said her former slave, 'but I shall never again be called a slattern, or a slave, or anything else that is not my own name. I am Lady Una, firstborn and only daughter of the eighty-first Lord of Stormhold, and the spells and terms you bound me with are over and done. Now, you will apologise to me, and you will call me by my right name, or I will – with enormous pleasure – devote the rest of my life to hunting you down and destroying every thing that you care for and every thing that you are.'

They looked at each other, then, and it was the old woman who looked away first.

'Then I must apologise for having called you a slattern, Lady Una,' she said, as if each word of it were bitter sawdust that she spat from her mouth.

Lady Una nodded. 'Good. And I believe that you owe me payment for my services, now my time with you is done,' she said. For these things have their rules. All things have rules.

***

The rain was still falling in gusts, then not falling for just long enough to lure people out from underneath their makeshift shelters, then raining on them once more. Tristran and Yvaine sat, damp and happy, beside a campfire, in the company of a motley assortment of creatures and people.

Tristran had asked if any of them knew the little hairy man he had met upon his travels, and had described him as well as he could. Several people acknowledged that they had met him in the past, although none had seen him at this market.

He found his hands twining, almost of their own volition,

into the star's wet hair. He wondered how it could have taken
him so long to realise how much he cared for her, and he told
her so, and she called him an idiot, and he declared that it
was the finest thing that ever a man had been called.

'So, where are we going once the market is done?' Tristran
asked the star.

'I do not know,' she said. 'But I have one obligation still to
discharge.'

'You do?'

'Yes,' she said. 'The topaz thing I showed you. I have to
give it to the right person. The last time the right person
came along, that innkeeper woman cut his throat, so I have
it still. But I wish it were gone.'

A woman's voice at his shoulder said, 'Ask her for what
she carries, Tristran Thorn.'

He turned, and stared into eyes the colour of meadow-
violets. 'You were the bird in the witch's caravan,' he told the
woman.

'When you were the dormouse, my son,' said the woman.
'I was the bird. But now I have my own form again, and my
time of servitude is over. Ask Yvaine for what she carries.
You have the right.'

He turned back to the star. 'Yvaine?'

She nodded, waiting.

'Yvaine, will you give me what you are carrying?'

She looked puzzled; then she reached inside her robe,
fumbled discreetly, and produced a large topaz stone on a
broken silver chain.

'It was your grandfather's,' said the woman to Tristran.
'You are the last male of the line of Stormhold. Put it about
your neck.'

Tristran did so; as he touched the ends of the silver chain
together they knit and mended as if they had never been
broken. 'It's very nice,' said Tristran, dubiously.

'It is the Power of Stormhold,' said his mother. 'There's no
one can argue with that. You are of the blood, and all of your

uncles are dead and gone. You will make a fine Lord of Stormhold.'

Tristran stared at her in honest puzzlement. 'But I have no wish to be a lord of anywhere,' he told her, 'or of anything, except perhaps my lady's heart.' And he took the star's hand in his, and he pressed it to his breast, and smiled.

The woman flicked her ears impatiently. 'In almost eighteen years, Tristran Thorn, I have not demanded one single thing of you. And now, the first simple little request that I make – the tiniest favour that I ask of you – you say me no. Now, I ask of you, Tristran, is that any way to treat your mother?'

'No, Mother,' said Tristran.

'Well,' she continued, slightly mollified, 'and I think it will do you young people good to have a home of your own, and for you to have an occupation. And if it does not suit you, you may leave, you know. There is no silver chain that will be holding you to the throne of Stormhold.'

And Tristran found this quite reassuring. Yvaine was less impressed, for she knew that silver chains come in all shapes and sizes; but she knew also that it would not be wise to begin her life with Tristran by arguing with his mother.

'Might I have the honour of knowing what you are called?' asked Yvaine, wondering if she was laying it on a bit thickly. Tristran's mother preened, and Yvaine knew that she was not.

'I am the Lady Una of Stormhold,' she said. Then she reached into a small bag, which hung from her side, and produced a rose made of glass, of a red so dark that it was almost black in the flickering firelight. 'It was my payment,' she said. 'For more than sixty years of servitude. It galled her to give it to me, but rules are rules, and she would have lost her magic and more if she had not settled up. Now, I plan to barter it for a palanquin to take us back to the Stormhold, for we must arrive in style. Oh, I have missed the Stormhold so badly. We must have bearers, and outriders, and perhaps an elephant – they are so imposing, nothing says "Get out of the way" quite like an elephant in the front . . .'

'No,' said Tristran.

'No?' said his mother.

'No,' repeated Tristran. '*You* may travel by palanquin, and elephant, and camel and all that, if you wish to, Mother. But Yvaine and I will make our own way there, and travel at our own speed.'

The Lady Una took a deep breath, and Yvaine decided that this argument was one that she would rather be somewhere else for, so she stood up, and told them that she would be back soon, that she needed a walk, and would not go wandering too far. Tristran looked at her with pleading eyes, but Yvaine shook her head: this was his fight to win, and he would fight it better if she were not there.

She limped through the darkening market, pausing beside a tent from which music and applause could be heard, and from which light spilled like warm, golden honey. She listened to the music, and she thought her own thoughts. It was there that a bent, white-haired old woman, glaucous-blind in one eye, hobbled over to the star, and bade her to stop a while and talk.

'About what?' asked the star.

The old woman, shrunk by age and time to little bigger than a child, held onto a stick as tall and bent as herself with palsied and swollen-knuckled hands. She stared up at the star with her good eye and her blue-milk eye, and she said, 'I came to fetch your heart back with me.'

'Is that so?' asked the star.

'Aye,' said the old woman. 'I nearly had it, at that, up in the mountain pass.' She cackled at the back of her throat at the memory. 'D'ye remember?' She had a large pack that sat like a hump on her back. A spiral ivory horn protruded from the pack, and Yvaine knew where she had seen that horn before.

'That was you?' asked the star of the tiny woman. 'You, with the knives?'

'Mm. That was me. But I squandered away all the youth I took for the journey. Every act of magic lost me a little of the youth I wore, and now I am older than I have ever been.'

'If you touch me,' said the star, 'lay but a finger on me, you will regret it forevermore.'

'If ever you get to be my age,' said the old woman, 'you will know all there is to know about regrets, and you will know that one more, here or there, will make no difference in the long run.' She snuffled the air. Her dress had once been red, but it seemed to have been much patched and taken up and faded over the years. It hung down from one shoulder, exposing a puckered scar that might have been many hundreds of years old. 'So what I want to know is why it is that I can no longer find you, in my mind. You are still there, just, but you are there like a ghost, a will o' the wisp. Not long ago you burned – your heart burned – in my mind like silver fire. But after that night in the inn it became patchy and dim, and now it is not there at all.'

Yvaine realised that she felt nothing but pity for the creature who had wanted her dead, so she said, 'Could it be that the heart that you seek is no longer my own?'

The old woman coughed. Her whole frame shook and spasmed with the retching effort of it.

The star waited for her to be done, and then she said, 'I have given my heart to another.'

'The boy? The one in the inn? With the unicorn?'

'Yes.'

'You should have let me take it back then, for my sisters and me. We could have been young again, well into the next age of the world. Your boy will break it, or waste it, or lose it. They all do.'

'Nonetheless,' said the star, 'he has my heart. I hope that your sisters will not be too hard on you, when you return to them without it.'

It was then that Tristran walked across to Yvaine, and took

her hand, and nodded to the old woman. 'All sorted out,' he said. 'Nothing to worry about.'

'And the palanquin?'

'Oh, Mother will be travelling by palanquin. I had to promise that we'd get to the Stormhold sooner or later, but we can take our time on the way. I think we should buy a couple of horses, and see the sights.'

'And your mother acceded to this?'

'In the end,' he said blithely. 'Anyway, sorry to interrupt.'

'We are almost done,' said Yvaine, and she turned back to the little old woman.

'My sisters will be harsh, but cruel,' said the old witch-queen. 'However, I appreciate the sentiment. You have a good heart, child. A pity it will not be mine.'

The star leaned down, then, and kissed the old woman on her wizened cheek, feeling the rough hairs on it scrape her soft lips.

Then the star and her true love walked away, toward the wall. 'Who was the old biddy?' asked Tristran. 'She seemed a bit familiar. Was anything wrong?'

'Nothing was wrong,' she told him. 'She was just someone I knew from the road.'

Behind them were the lights of the market, the lanterns and candles and witch-lights and fairy glitter, like a dream of the night sky brought down to earth. In front of them, across the meadow, on the other side of the gap in the wall, now guardless, was the town of Wall. Oil lamps and gas lamps and candles glowed in the windows of the houses of the village. To Tristran, then, they seemed as distant and unknowable as the world of the Arabian Nights.

He looked upon the lights of Wall for what he knew (it came to him then with certainty) was the last time. He stared at them for some time and said nothing, the fallen star by his side. And then he turned away, and together they began to walk toward the East.

Epilogue

In Which Several Endings May Be Discerned

I t was considered by many to be one of the greatest days in the history of the Stormhold, the day that Lady Una, long lost and believed to be dead (having been stolen, as an infant, by a witch), returned to the mountain land. There were celebrations and fireworks and rejoicings (official and otherwise) for weeks after her palanquin arrived in a procession led by three elephants.

The joy of the inhabitants of Stormhold and all its dominions was raised to levels hitherto unparalleled when the Lady Una announced that, in her time away, she had given birth to a son, who, in the absence and presumed death of the last two of her brothers, was the next heir to the throne. Indeed, she told them, he already wore the Power of Stormhold about his neck.

He and his new bride would come to them soon, though the Lady Una could be no more specific about the date of their arrival than this, and it appeared to irk her. In the meantime, and in their absence, the Lady Una announced that she would rule the Stormhold as regent. Which she did, and did well, and the dominions on and about Mount

Huon prospered and flourished under her command.

It was three more years before two travel-stained wanderers arrived, dusty and footsore, in the town of Cloudsrange, in the lower reaches of the Stormhold proper, and they took a room in an inn, and sent for hot water and a tin bath. They stayed at the inn for several days, conversing with the other customers and guests. On the last night of their stay, the woman, whose hair was so fair it was almost white, and who walked with a limp, looked at the man, and said, 'Well?'

'Well,' he said. 'Mother certainly seems to be doing an excellent job of reigning.'

'Just as you,' she told him, tartly, 'would do every bit as well, if you took the throne.'

'Perhaps,' he admitted. 'And it certainly seems like it would be a nice place to end up, eventually. But there are so many places we have not yet seen. So many people still to meet. Not to mention all the wrongs to right, villains to vanquish, sights to see, all that. You know.'

She smiled, wryly. 'Well,' she said, 'at least we shall not be bored. But we had better leave your mother a note.'

And so it was that the Lady Una of Stormhold was brought a sheet of paper by an innkeeper's lad. The sheet was sealed with sealing wax, and the Lady Una questioned the boy closely about the travellers – a man and his wife – before she broke the seal and read the letter. It was addressed to her, and after the salutations, it read:

Have been unavoidably detained by the world.
Expect us when you see us.

It was signed by Tristran, and beside his signature was a fingerprint, which glittered and glimmered and shone when the shadows touched it as if it had been dusted with tiny stars.

With which, there being nothing else that she could do about it, Una had to content herself.

It was another five years after that before the two travellers finally returned for good to the mountain fastness. They were dusty and tired and dressed in rags and tatters, and were at first, and to the shame of the entire land, treated as vagabonds and rogues; it was not until the man displayed the topaz stone that hung about his neck that he was recognized as the Lady Una's only son.

The investiture and subsequent celebrations went on for almost a month, after which the young eighty-second Lord of Stormhold got on with the business of ruling. He made as few decisions as possible, but those he made were wise ones, even if the wisdom was not always apparent at the time. He was valiant in battle, though his left hand was scarred and of little use, and a cunning strategist; he led his people to victory against the Northern Goblins when they closed the passes to travellers; he forged a lasting peace with the Eagles of the High Crags, a peace that remains in place until this day.

His wife, the Lady Yvaine, was a fair woman from distant parts (although no one was ever entirely certain quite which ones). When she and her husband first arrived at Stormhold, she took herself a suite of rooms in one of the highest peaks of the citadel, a suite that had long been abandoned as unusable by the palace and its staff; its roof had collapsed in a rock fall a thousand years earlier. No one else had wished to use the rooms, for they were open to the sky, and the stars and the moon shone down upon them so brightly through the thin mountain air that it seemed one could simply reach out and hold them in one's hand.

Tristran and Yvaine were happy together. Not forever-after, for Time, the thief, eventually takes all things into his dusty storehouse, but they were happy, as these things go, for a long while. And then Death came in the night, and whispered her secret into the ear of the eighty-second Lord of Stormhold, and he nodded his grey head and he said nothing more, and his people took his remains to the Hall of Ancestors where they lie to this day.

After Tristran's death, there were those who claimed that he was a member of the Fellowship of the Castle, and was instrumental in breaking the power of the Unseelie Court. But the truth of that, as so much else, died with him, and has never been established, neither one way nor another.

Yvaine became the Lady of Stormhold, and proved a better monarch, in peace and in war, than any would have dared to hope. She did not age as her husband had aged, and her eyes remained as blue, her hair as golden-white, and – as the free citizens of the Stormhold would have occasional cause to discover – her temper as quick to flare as on the day that Tristran first encountered her in the glade beside the pool.

She walks with a limp to this day, although no one in the Stormhold would ever remark upon it, any more than they dare remark upon the way she glitters and shines, upon occasion, in the darkness.

They say that each night, when the duties of state permit, she climbs, on foot, and limps, alone, to the highest peak of the palace, where she stands for hour after hour, seeming not to notice the cold peak winds. She says nothing at all, but simply stares upward into the dark sky and watches, with sad eyes, the slow dance of the infinite stars.

Acknowledgements

First and foremost, my thanks to Charles Vess. He is the nearest thing we have today to the great Victorian fairy painters, and without his art as an inspiration none of these words would exist. Every time I finished a chapter I phoned him up and read it to him, and he listened patiently and he chuckled in all the right places.

My thanks to Jenny Lee, Karen Berger, Paul Levitz, Merrilee Heifetz, Lou Aronica, Jennifer Hershey and Tia Maggini: each of them helped make this book a reality.

I owe an enormous debt to Hope Mirrlees, Lord Dunsany, James Branch Cabell and C. S. Lewis, wherever they may currently be, for showing me that fairy stories were for adults too.

Tori lent me a house, and I wrote the first chapter in it, and all she asked in exchange was that I make her a tree.

There were people who read it as it was being written, and who told me what I was doing right and what I was doing wrong. It's not their fault if I didn't listen. My thanks in particular to Amy Horsting, Lisa Henson, Diana Wynne Jones, Chris Bell and Susanna Clarke.

My wife Mary and my assistant Lorraine did more than their share of work on this book, for they typed the first few chapters from my handwritten draft, and I cannot thank them enough.

The kids, to be frank, were absolutely no help at all, and I truly don't think I'd ever have it any other way.

Neil Gaiman

EXclusive Material

Contents

Author's Preface to
WALL: A Prologue

*S*tardust was the sequel to a novel I haven't written, and that I'm not sure I'll ever write. Maybe one day.

Wall came first, the little town on the border between England and Faerie. And with it came an idea for a story, set in the here and now, about a fortysomething romance novelist who returns from America and settles in the village of Wall. It would have been a love story, of a sort, I think, magical and odd, but always set firmly on this side of the Wall.

I wrote the first chapter, which was set a long time before the rest of the book.

And then, for whatever reason, I stopped.

Late one night, a year or so later, in a desert, I watched a star fall like a burning jewel and, in a moment, the whole opening of *Stardust* presented itself to me.

I started to write it. I bought a pen specially, feeling that it might be a good idea to write a book in fountain pen, an affectation that I'm now saddled with. I had enormous fun creating the Victorian ancestors of the people who live in

Wall in recent times – the Thornes and the Hempstocks and the rest. Mr Bromios is still serving excellent wines in the *Seventh Pie*, waiting for Jenny Kerton to arrive.

(People are seen reading books by Jenny Kerton in *American Gods*, by the way.)

I may write *Wall* one day or I may not, and I may use this prologue or I may not (although I suspect in each case I shall) but either way it was what I wrote all those years ago, and was the place the story began.

It has only been published once before, in 1999's *A Fall of Stardust*, which was a portfolio of illustrations by various artists done to raise money for medical treatment for artist Charles Vess's wife Karen, following a nasty car accident. It also contained the only short story written about Wall by anyone else – Susanna Clarke's delightful tale of how Lord Wellington regained his horse.

(The other story set in the world of Stardust that I still intend to tell explains how and why Tristran Thorne went to Hell in a hot air balloon.)

I hope you'll enjoy it.

Melbourne, Australia, 15 July, 2005

Wall

A Prologue

It wasn't black and white, not when you saw it up close. Jenny held her breath, frightened of scaring the bird away.

Its long tail was raised clear off the ground, and it strutted inquisitively across the neatly trimmed grass of the Kertons' lawn.

Jenny stared at the magpie in fascination. Its belly and the flash on its wings were pure white, but the black that covered its head and back, wingtips, and tail, was far from black when seen from close to: she could make out red and violet and green in its tail, blue and green in its wings, and overlaying all was a pure viridian sheen.

One for sorrow, thought Jenny.

She was twelve.

She stood on the grass in her bare feet, feeling the turf between her toes, smelling the evening air. It had rained earlier, and the grass was still wet.

That's a pity, she thought. I don't want to have to be sad.

There was a whirring from above her, and, as if in answer

to her thought, another magpie fluttered down from the autumn sky.

Two for joy, thought Jenny. That's better.

The two magpies walked around each other like fat men in evening dress, eyeing each other as if they were wondering which of them was to begin the conversation.

The early evening air was quiet. The sky was overcast, the air was grey and cool. Jenny was wearing her print cotton skirt, and a white cotton blouse.

It was Friday, the Eighth of November, 1963, and tomorrow was her birthday.

Whirr.

A third magpie joined the other two.

Three for a girl, thought Jenny. That must be me.

She wondered if she'd feel any different when she was thirteen. She doubted it. Jenny distrusted birthdays; despite the presents, she was wary of them. You go to sleep one age, wake up another, with no say in the matter.

Tomorrow she'd be a teenager.

Whirr.

It landed awkwardly, hopped to the side to regain its balance.

Four for a boy. She thought about that, staring at the four birds the while, then shook her head. No, no boys. Only her brothers.

The magpies were now ignoring each other, industriously scanning the wet grass, occasionally picking at something with their curved black beaks.

They weren't as big as she had thought, either, seen up close. Most of the length was in the tail. The magpies' tails bobbed up and down as they circled on the patch of lawn in front of her.

She had read a book a week or so back, set in a girls' boarding school: Alison, the scholarship girl, was blamed for the theft of some rings belonging to Marjorie, the snobby girl and captain of the lacrosse team. In the last chapter the rings were discovered in a magpie's nest, however, and when Marjorie had sprained her ankle Alison had led the lacrosse team to victory.

Jenny wondered if magpies really stole shiny things.

She wondered how long she could stand there without moving. She really didn't want to scare them away, but she was beginning to get a cramp in her left thigh.

Whirr.

Whirr.

Two more magpies. One fairly small – a young one. Jenny ran through the rhyme in her head. Five for silver. Six for gold.

Did that mean she was going to be rich, one day? Jenny wasn't sure if she'd like that.

Six magpies.

She could hear, some way off, her brothers calling to each other in the woods behind the house. She hoped desperately that their game wouldn't bring them any closer, that they wouldn't scare the birds away.

Somehow she knew that you didn't get many moments like this in your life: moments when you knew, without any doubt, that you were alive, when you felt the air in your lungs and the wet grass beneath your feet and the cotton on your skin; moments when you were completely in the present, when neither the past nor the future mattered.

She tried to slow her breathing, hoping somehow to make this moment last for ever.

The magpies had stopped circling, had stopped hunting and pecking. One of them was staring at her, its head tipped slightly to one side. The others were just . . .

They were *waiting*.

Jenny waited with them. She wriggled her bare toes in the wet grass.

She couldn't hear her brothers any longer. They must have gone into the house, or further into the woods.

Whirr.

This magpie was huge.

It's the last of them, she thought. 'Seven for a secret never to be told.' It's the end of the rhyme.

She stared at it in awe: it must have measured almost two feet from the tip of its beak to the end of its tail. And the *colours*. There were colours in the feathers of its wings and tail she wasn't even sure she could name. The other six magpies shuffled and hopped around it, until they had arranged themselves in a rough semicircle, all facing Jenny.

Jenny looked at the magpies, in the cool of the autumn twilight.

The magpies looked back at her. They seemed to be waiting for something.

'Seven for a secret, never to be told.'

She had always counted the magpies they had passed in the car, but had never seen more than three together, before now.

'All right,' she said to the birds. 'What's the secret?'

For a moment she thought that she had scared them, that the action of speaking might somehow have broken the spell; but the birds didn't move.

The last magpie stared up at her. It put its head on one side, as if it were weighing her up, as if she were a shiny ring, and it was trying to decide whether she was worth taking back to its nest.

'You're going to Wall,' the magpie said, in a rough, metallic voice.

Jenny opened her mouth to speak, and hesitated.

'Where?' she asked. 'Where am I going?'

The smallest of the birds walked forward. 'But it's a secret,' it told her. 'You can't tell anyone.'

'But—'

She never finished. As one, the birds took off, and it seemed like the air was filled with black and white (and green and blue), as if she could hear nothing but the beating of wings. She took a step back in alarm, heart thumping in her breast.

The birds were gone.

The magic was over, and suddenly Jenny felt sick. Her stomach felt tight, and her heart was beating too fast. Panic took her, and she didn't understand why.

She ran across the damp lawn, into the house.

Her mother was in the kitchen, sitting at the table stringing runner beans. 'Jennifer? You all right, love?'

Jenny nodded, without saying anything, and ran into the hall. She felt like her stomach was pinching, hard, inside; she felt nauseous, and strange.

She went up the stairs, two at a time, and into the bathroom at the top of the stairs. She locked the door behind her, leaned against it heavily. The pain was getting worse, and she was feeling dizzy.

She sat down, slowly, easing herself on to the cold lino.

She closed her eyes.

In her head the magpies were still flying, black eyes staring down at her, wings flapping in slow motion, huge black and white birds trapped in time, held behind her eyes.

She felt something wet between her legs.

Jenny opened her eyes, pulled at her skirt, uncovering her thin white legs until she could see her white cotton panties. A red stain had begun to spread across the crotch.

She shivered and closed her eyes again.

You can't go back, she thought. It's the dividing line. I'm not a little girl any more.

Maybe that's what the magpies were trying to tell me.

She put tissue paper in her panties, and went back downstairs, to talk to her mother, to find out what to do now.

Nothing would ever be the same again.

She knew that now.

Jenny Kerton never forgot that day, although, as time went on, the time in the bathroom, and her mother's explanation, and the fitting of the sanitary pad, and the bitter taste of the aspirin her mother dissolved in a glass of water for her, gradually took prominence over the event that preceded them.

And after thirty years had passed, all that remained in her memory was the sheen of green and violet on a magpie's wings: the knowledge that, when you got up close, it wasn't simply black and white.

An Interview with Neil Gaiman

How much truth is there in fairy tales?

I think all fairy tales are true on a huge level, on the macro level; if not on the micro level. There's the line that I quote at the beginning of *Coraline*, my children's novel, which is from GK Chesterton. He says that it's not that fairy tales are true, they're more than true. And they're not true because they tell us dragons exist, since all children know in their hearts that dragons exist; they're true because they tell us that dragons can be beaten.

And I think that's the biggest and most important part of every fairy tale. They tell us big true things that aren't necessarily small and specific.

Fairy tales *became* for children, they didn't start out like that. Tolkien's analogy was that of the furniture in the nursery. The furniture didn't start out as nursery furniture; it was built for adults and they sent it to the nursery when it got old and out of fashion.

In the case of the Brothers Grimm, they were collecting and publishing their stories, and they believed they were publishing them for adults. It wasn't until they started getting letters from adults who had bought these stories and started reading them to their children and felt they were improper that the Grimms began changing the stories.

So Rapunzel, in the first edition of the Grimms' fairy tale, says to the witch, 'Why is my belly swelling? My clothes no longer fit.' Whereas by the third edition, the witch at that point knows that she's been seeing a young man because Rapunzel says something like, 'Old Mother, you are not as heavy as the prince.'

They started cleaning it up pretty early on. And of course Charles Perrault, in the 17th century, when he told the tales for the French, was again cleaning them up and also adding little morals.

I don't think fairy stories ever started out as stories for children; they started out as stories to be told to people. I also think that Faerie is the perfect metaphor for a lot of places, and for a lot of things and a lot of ideas, and it's also a wonderful place to set stories. And in *Stardust* I loved contrasting it with the bowler-hatted Victorians.

What's your favourite fairy tale?

I'm very fond of 'The Juniper Tree', a really strange Grimms' fairy tale with cannibalism in it.

My favourite expression of a fairy tale is probably Jean Cocteau's film *Beauty and the Beast*, which I love. I recently showed it to my kids, and was astonished that they watched it all through despite the fact it was subtitled.

Which side of the Wall do you live on?

I suppose in terms of where I live, it's firmly on our side of the Wall. But it's probably close enough to the Wall that some things don't work when the wind's in the right direction.

How could you kill a unicorn?

Well, because I wanted to have a book in which some people weren't safe.

I loved my unicorn; I was very, very fond of that unicorn, and I was sorry that it died. But on the other hand it seemed at the time a really interesting way to try and remind people that this wasn't necessarily a fairy tale for children. That and having one rude word in incredibly small type.

If you fell foul of a witch, what animal would you be turned into?

I think I could be a perfectly decent cat. I've been around cats enough to know what the rules of being a cat are. When all else fails, wash. And I think I could master the thing that cats do, where they stalk away pretending they meant to do whatever it was in the first place; showing their wounded dignity.

We know Tori Amos is the tree. Are there any other characters in STARDUST that were based on people you know?

I don't think so. I don't think I put any others in. It's actually one of the very few times I've put a friend into a book.

I showed Tori some of the original illustrations that Charles Vess did – this was before I ever set pen to paper – and she looked at it and said, 'I want to be a tree.'

I said, 'OK, I'll make you a tree.' And so she sang a song about Neil making her a tree, and for four or five years people would come up to me and say, 'What does that mean?'

I'd say, 'Wait and see,' and finally *Stardust* came out and I'd made her a tree.

Reading-group Discussion Questions

1. What traditional fairy tales and characters does *Stardust* draw on, and how have they been given a new twist? What do you think about the underlying darkness in fairy tales? Does anyone live happily ever after?

2. Tristran begins the novel as an everyman protagonist set an apparently impossible task. How does his quest alter him? What changes occur when he leaves Wall, and which aspects of his character flourish in the land of Faerie? How does Yvaine's perception of him change during their journey together, and why?

3. What techniques does Neil Gaiman use to create the different worlds in *Stardust*? How does he use language to make the narrative and description lyrical and original? What do the many vivid secondary characters add to the overall impression of the story, and who stands out particularly strongly?

4. How do the female characters take charge in *Stardust*? What are the relationships between them, and how do they demonstrate their power? What do they have in common?

5. How is the humour and comedy of the novel countered by the sad or poignant moments? Which episodes were you moved by? Who did you feel particularly sympathetic towards, and why?

6. What do you consider to be the main themes of *Stardust*? What does Tristran's journey to find his 'heart's desire' teach him? What is the significance of his choice at the end? How does the novel explore magic, romance and the battle between good and evil?

Neverwhere

Under the streets of London there's a place most people could never even dream of. A city of monsters and saints, murderers and angels, knights in armour and pale girls in black velvet. This is the city of the people who have fallen between the cracks.

Richard Mayhew, a young businessman, is going to find out more than enough about this other London. A single act of kindness catapults him out of his workaday existence and into a world that is at once eerily familiar and utterly bizarre. And a strange destiny awaits him down here, beneath his native city: NEVERWHERE.

'Exuberantly inventive . . . a postmodernist punk *Faerie Queen*' *Kirkus Reviews*

978 0 7553 2280 0

review

Now you can buy any of these other bestselling books by **Neil Gaiman** from your bookshop or *direct from his publisher.*

FREE P&P AND UK DELIVERY
(Overseas and Ireland £3.50 per book)

Fragile Things	£7.99
Anansi Boys	£7.99
American Gods	£7.99
Neverwhere	£7.99
Smoke and Mirrors	£7.99

TO ORDER SIMPLY CALL THIS NUMBER

01235 400 414

or visit our website: www.headline.co.uk

Prices and availability subject to change without notice.